PROPERTY OF GARY

Novels by Jim Braly

Johnny's War

Invade Rinse Repeat

Published June 2014

"Property of Gary" received its first public reading on April 1, 2014, at Stonehenge Studios in Portland, Oregon, at a meeting of PDX Playwrights.

Property of Gary: A play / 1st edition

ISBN 978-0-9837747-3-0

Printed in the United States of America

Published by Cascadia Press
cascadiapress@gmail.com
Portland, Oregon

Cover photograph by Michael Deschenes

PROPERTY OF GARY

A play

Jim Braly

Characters

GARY, artistic, volatile, tattoos, mid-thirties

WOMAN, glasses, dark hair, tattoos, early-thirties

FATHER'S VOICE
(**Note**: Father makes a brief appearance in silhouette, Scene 13, and could be played by the actor who plays Gary.)

MOTHER'S VOICE

JUDGE'S VOICE

Settings

Interior of a house
Hospital bed
Rollaway bed
Courtroom chair

Time

Present day

Act I

Scenes 1 through 10

Act II

Scenes 11 through 18

Act I

Scene 1

In the dark, before rise

A loud, obnoxious buzzing.

At rise

The house.

Upstage, Woman cowers in an open kitchen behind a dining table, which is tipped over, with one broken leg, and a steak knife plunged into its top. It is surrounded by mismatched kitchen chairs. Downstage are a "coffee table," a couch, a small television, an overstuffed chair, and a fireplace. The entrance to the house is upstage. There is also a doorway to an offstage bedroom.

Gary stands next to the "coffee table," which is actually a wooden door set up on blocks. We know it's a door because the door knobs are still there. Upon the "table" are a cheap tin vase holding a single red rose, a bottle of alcohol disinfectant, a rag, a pair of rubber gloves, and a Xanax pill in a shallow dish.

Gary holds the source of the psychotic buzzing: A tattoo gun with its vibrating needle.

GARY   Come on. Get over here.

WOMAN   Please, Gary, no.

GARY   See, that's the problem. You have put your finger right on the problem. You don't please me. You don't even try.

WOMAN   I do try. I try really hard … please.

GARY   I don't think so. You need something to help you focus. Something permanent. A permanent reminder of who you belong to. Who *do* you belong to?

WOMAN   You.

GARY   For how long?

WOMAN   Forever.

GARY   Do you mean that?

WOMAN   Of course I do, baby. I love you. Please turn off the needle. You don't need to do this. You're always in my mind. I'm always thinking about you. I belong to you, and only you.

(Gary turns off the tattoo gun and places it on the door knob "coffee table." Sweet relief from the awful noise.)

GARY   See, the thing is, I hear you say it, but I don't *feel* it. That's what I'm having a really hard time with. It's hard for me to believe you when I *know* you and that guy from —

WOMAN   I told you! Over and over again. *I didn't!* NOTHING HAPPENED!

GARY   I know what you said. But I also know what I saw … I saw the way you looked at him.

WOMAN   He gave me a ride home, Gary. That's what you saw. That's all it was. I swear. My car wouldn't start. He gave me a ride home. A simple ride home.

GARY   Come here. Why are you hiding over there? Have you got something to hide? Come here, and we'll talk about it. Have a little talk.

WOMAN   We *have* talked about it. We've talked about it for a week. I swear to you, I have not said a word to that guy since he gave me the ride home. That's all it was. A ride home. My car wouldn't start.

GARY   And why was that? Tell me: Why wouldn't your car start? What did you do to it?

WOMAN   Nothing. I turned the key and it didn't start. The battery was dead.

GARY   Maybe *Delbert* drained *your* battery. I'll bet *you* started up, though, no problem … Aren't you going to tell me his name isn't Delbert?

WOMAN   Gary, I don't know what his name is.

GARY   I doubt that. His name is *Dennis*. I checked.

WOMAN   *(sniffling and crying)*   It was a ride home … That's all it was … A ride home.

GARY   Don't cry, baby doll. I don't want you to cry. I love you so much … But I want you to admit what you did … We can't move on until you admit what you did. Do you understand that? Isn't that perfectly logical? Unless *you* do some changing, we're stuck.

WOMAN   I didn't … do … *anything!*

GARY   Maybe you didn't … Maybe you just laid there … Maybe *Dennis* did all the work. Is that it? You're pretty good at just lying there. That's something you know how to do. Lie there. And *lie* about it. But we can move past this. I know we can. It won't take much. In your heart, I think you know that you're the only one for me and I'm the only one for you. But I

don't think *Dennis* knows that. That's the real problem … So let's make sure, the next time he's eyeball-
ing your back, the next time he gives you a *"ride,"* let's
make sure he understands. OK? Is that too much to
ask? … Now come on over here and get on the table.

WOMAN Please … no.

> (Gary advances on Woman, grabs her
> by the legs, and drags her toward the
> downstage "coffee table.")

GARY YOU DON'T TELL ME NO! YOU *NEVER*
SAY NO TO ME! You understand?

> (Woman howls. She grabs a chair and pulls
> it along. When they get to the "coffee table,"
> Gary lets go. Woman curls up on the floor.)

GARY This is going to fix everything. We're *both*
changing now. This is going to solve all of our problems. This will bring us together. It'll be better than
having a kid … We've just got to make sure everybody knows who you belong to … Now come on …
It's not like you don't have any ink. You know how
this goes. It only hurts for a little while. And then
you're proud of it.

> (A beat.)

WOMAN What's it going to say?

GARY I can tell you what it's not gonna say. It's *not*
gonna say, "California here I come."

> (No response from Woman.)

GARY GET ON THE TABLE!

> (Gary immediately cools off. He strokes
> Woman's hair. She recoils at his touch.)

GARY   Woman, you're just wasting my time and yours. This is gonna be the best tatt you ever got. I'm gonna make it beautiful … Kinda gothic. But clear, classy gothic … Let's make sure *Dennis* gets the message. I hate it when you can't read it. What's the point? Where's the message in that? I see sloppy work like that, I don't want to kill the messenger, I want to kill the artist.

(Gary grabs Woman by the hair
and starts to pull her up.)

WOMAN   You're hurting me!

(Gary lets go; she slumps to the floor.)

GARY   YOU'RE HURTING *ME!*

(A beat.)

(Gary snatches the vase off the "coffee table" and throws it against the wall. The vase clatters onto the floor.)

GARY   See what you made me do? There goes your rose. Is that what you want? Now go clean that up, and then we'll get you on the table.

(Woman doesn't move or speak. Gary waits. Then he lunges down and lifts Woman to her feet. A struggle begins. Woman shrieks and flails, but she is no match for Gary's strength. He gags her with his hand until she goes silent and quits resisting.)

GARY   OK … Are we cool now? Do we understand each other?

(Woman gives a reluctant nod yes.)

GARY All right, then. Let's just everybody relax … I'm gonna let go … I'll take a step back … And then I'm gonna give you something, a present, a little gift … a Xanax, a whole one, because I know you better than anybody ever has. Because I care. No pain, stay sane.

(Gary releases his grip on Woman
and moves away.)

(He turns to the door knob "coffee table"
and picks up the dish holding the Xanax.
He offers it to Woman. She's been swallow-
ing bitter pills for a long time. This night is
just one more. She puts the Xanax on her
tongue. Down it goes. She anticipates the
relief that will make life bearable.)

GARY You know what to do.

(Woman lies face down on the "coffee
table." She latches onto the door knob
with a death grip. Gary moves in and
positions the tattoo gun, the bottle of
disinfectant, and the rag next to her.)

(Gary rips open Woman's button-up
blouse in the back. He unhooks her
bra.)

GARY A little alcohol … Smooth and cool … Wouldn't want you to get an infection. You've got a nice back. Pretty good skin. Not the best I've ever seen, but it's all right. I'll work around the freckles. Maybe include them in the design. Now just relax. You seem a little tense.

(Gary puts on the rubber gloves.
He pours disinfectant on the rag
and swabs Woman's back.)

(Gary picks up the tattoo gun, flicks a switch, and the stillness is shattered by the awful buzzing. He begins to ink the tattoo.)

(Woman's shoulders knot up; she feels sharp pain from the needle.)

(Lights slowly fade to black as Gary works, but the buzzing continues. It finally fades to silence just before the dialogue begins in Scene 2.)

(**Set change note:** During the blackout between Scene 1 and Scene 2, the door knob "coffee table" is replaced with a normal coffee table. The dining table is restored to its upright position, its leg is fixed, and the knife is removed.)

Scene 2

The house.

Before lights come up, as set changes are made, we hear dialogue from outside the house as Gary and Woman walk down the street and arrive at the front door.

GARY It feels wrong that it's so nice out. What's with this amazing weather? Where's the rain?

WOMAN Something's definitely wrong. It's like summer forgot to get out of town. Maybe it's global warming. Good for us, bad for Pago Pago.

GARY   Pago Pago? What's that? What's that?

WOMAN   It's either a South Seas island or a Polynesian spaghetti sauce.

GARY   I'd *go* there, but I'm kind of iffy about the sauce … So, this is my place.

WOMAN   A bungalow. Cute.

GARY   It's small, only one bedroom, but I prefer to call it cozy … You wanna come in for a little minute?

WOMAN   I guess so.

(Key in lock. Door opens. Hand flicks
a wall switch. Lights up.)

(Gary and Woman enter.)

GARY   All is revealed.

WOMAN   Looks fairly normal.

GARY   I'd say I have a pretty good grasp on normal. Thanks for noticing.

(Woman strolls around, evaluating. She bumps
into the normal coffee table, steps around it.)

WOMAN   I just meant, you know, it's not scary. Some guys, when you open their closet, you have no idea what you're going to find.

GARY   You're talking about clothes, right?

WOMAN   Yes. Awful, terrible stuff — like leisure suits that haven't been dry-cleaned since 1982. Like platform disco shoes. And occasionally, the skeletons.

GARY   (*shivers*)   You're giving me goosebumps.

WOMAN   The leisure suits, the disco shoes, or the skeletons?

GARY   Oh, the suits and shoes. Definitely the suits and shoes.

WOMAN   So you're not afraid of skeletons?

GARY   I never really thought about it, but I guess it's a good idea to stay away from dark, enclosed spaces full of bones.

WOMAN   I took an acting class one time. The main thing I remember is, "Never go to an audition in an unfinished basement."

GARY   Is insurance just your day job? You're actually an actress?

WOMAN   Only if you count everyday life. No, that class was years ago. I did it on a whim.

GARY   I like whims.

WOMAN   It depends on how they turn out.

(Woman notices a painting on the wall.)

WOMAN   This is interesting. I'd hate to meet the tortured soul who committed this roar/shock to canvas.

GARY   You already did. That's a piece of mine.

WOMAN   Oops. I have a big, clumsy mouth. I meant "the artist with a flair for wild brush strokes and unusual color combinations."

GARY   Thanks. I think.

WOMAN   Seriously, you painted this?

GARY   I should have pleaded the Fifth.

WOMAN   So this would explain how you became a tattoo artist?

GARY   Not exactly. I studied art, but only for about five minutes.

WOMAN   In college?

GARY   No.

WOMAN   In high school? A magnet school or something?

GARY   I don't know if you'd call it a school … Maybe … I definitely learned some stuff in there. There *was* a magnetic pull on some of the guys.

WOMAN   But how do you go from "five minutes" of studying art to doing tattoos on real people?

GARY   You sure do ask a lotta questions. Are you one of those girls that has to know everything?

WOMAN   There must have been some steps in between. Getting from Point A to Point B. Or Point X, Y or Z.

GARY   I guess there were.

WOMAN   What was the first tattoo you ever did?

GARY   You want to see it?

WOMAN   You saved a picture?

GARY   I've got the actual ink.

WOMAN   Huh?

GARY   *(pats his left bicep)*   Right here.

(A confused look from Woman.)

GARY   On my arm.

WOMAN   You tattooed *yourself?*

GARY   The first time is really hard. You don't know how to do it because you've never done it, and you can't find anybody to do it on.

WOMAN   You can't get experience without a job, and you can't get a job without experience.

GARY   Right. How does anybody get beyond Point A? How did you start working in an insurance office?

WOMAN   Basically, I knew how to type. And I don't know if I'd call it working. It's more like typing claim forms into a computer. And then running a program that rejects the claim because it has an asterisk instead of a dash in column 17. And then calling tech support after the computer crashes and loses the claim form database when somebody's house burns down or they crash their car or something else bad happens.

GARY   So if an oil train blows up and destroys the north side of town, you're going to be really busy.

WOMAN   Something big like that, they'll probably lay me off and hire temps, people who know even less than I do. But I don't think we cover oil train explosions. Oh, maybe. It might be under the "act of God" clause.

GARY   God is a funny guy, kind of a warped sense of humor. He's like a standup comedian.

WOMAN   More of a heckler, if you ask me … So, are you going to show me your first tattoo?

GARY   If you promise not to laugh or heckle.

WOMAN   Why would I laugh or heckle?

GARY   It's not the world's best tattoo. In fact, it might be the world's worst tattoo.

WOMAN   Everybody's got to start somewhere. When you don't know what you're getting into. Point A.

(Gary rolls up the sleeve of his shirt.
Woman looks at the tattoo.)

WOMAN   Wow ... it's ... very ... interesting. It's very blue.

GARY   There's a fancy word for that, mono-something. All we had was blue ink.

WOMAN   You couldn't get any other colors?

GARY   Sometimes we had black, but usually blue. Ink was hard to come by. You had to get your hands on a ballpoint pen. Once in a while, somebody would have some purple or red. That was really expensive.

WOMAN   Wait ... A pen? *Sometimes* you could get different colors? I don't think I'm following you.

GARY   Can you tell what it is?

WOMAN   Uhm, let's see ... a brain?

GARY   No, but good guess.

WOMAN   A cauliflower?

GARY   A *blue* cauliflower?

WOMAN   It could be impressionist.

GARY   Impressionist?

WOMAN   Uh, you know, that style, not a lot of detail, just kind of giving ... an impression?

GARY   Oh. Maybe I'm an impressionist. OK, one more chance.

WOMAN   Well, let's see, it's round ... it's blue ... is it ... a ...

GARY   Blue blob? Yes, it's a blue blob.

WOMAN   It has character.

GARY   Character is overrated. I keep it covered. It's not a good advertisement for the work I do now, so I should get it removed, but you know how it is. Your first tattoo is your "first," so ... *(a sheepish shrug)* ... Besides, removal is *really* painful.

WOMAN   So I've heard. Getting inked is bad enough. I always take half a Xanax. Or a whole one if I'm going to have to lie there for five or six hours.

GARY   We didn't have anything like that. No drugs. This is totally DIY. I had to use a staple.

WOMAN   A staple? You mean like stapling paper together?

GARY   Exactly. The staple has a sharp steel point — sharp enough to puncture the skin. That's all you really need. Dip the point into the ink you got from the pen and jab yourself a few hundred times — no, a few *thousand* times.

WOMAN   Ouch!

GARY   My arm swole up to twice its size. It got infected and some of the flesh rotted away. Which kind of explains why it's a tattoo underneath a scar. Makes it harder to see the detail. Not that there's a lot of detail. Lesson learned. Don't use an unsterilized staple to do your own stick 'n' poke. Also, make sure you get more than one staple. You'd be surprised how tough skin is. The staple gets dull after five minutes. Skin can really take a beating.

WOMAN   But a staple? Why use a staple?

GARY   It's all we could get. There weren't any needles ... I did this in prison.

(Awkward silence.)

GARY   But I've changed. I'm very different now.

WOMAN   Sorry. Did I have a look on my face? I wasn't expecting that.

GARY   Neither was I.

WOMAN   What do people say when you tell them?

GARY   I've never told anybody. Before now.

WOMAN   Gee, I feel kind of … honored.

GARY   It's not something you just blurt out to people. The first thing outta their mouth would be "what were you in for?"

WOMAN   I can see where they might be … interested in knowing that little detail.

GARY   Yeah, well, if I did tell somebody that I did four years, and they asked me why, I'd say I hit a rough patch. I wrote some checks I shouldn't have. I'm really bad at math. That's why I'm an artist.

WOMAN   They put you in prison for writing bad checks? In this state, you can kill a pedestrian in a crosswalk and only get a slap on the wrist. Or nothing at all if you don't drive off.

GARY   I did it. I got caught. I took responsibility. I did the time.

WOMAN   What's prison like?

GARY   Your world is small. You have a lot of people telling you what to do and when to do it.

WOMAN   Are you talking about prison or my job?

GARY   How long are *you* in for?

WOMAN   Life, I guess.

GARY   We're all in some kind of big house. It owns you. You don't appreciate freedom till you don't have it. When I first got out, I had this idea for a piece of performance art. A guy sitting in a chair making license plates. That's all he's doing. Sitting there. For eight hours. Making license plates. Running a noisy stamping machine. At the end of his shift, he stands up, goes to a giant time clock, he struggles to get his giant time card into the giant clock, and he punches out. Then he shoots himself in the head with a giant gun … He *punches out.* In a big way. He's free.

WOMAN   Wow … that's dark.

GARY   You think so?

WOMAN   I kind of do. And isn't that kind of long? Would anybody go see a show that's eight hours long? You'd need really comfortable chairs.

GARY   What if I covered myself in chocolate?

WOMAN   You mean instead of the giant gun at the end? Instead of the giant bullet in the brain?

GARY   I was kinda kidding, but maybe you're right. That might take the edge off. Give it a twist. Suddenly the vibe changes. Maybe it becomes comedy instead of suicide.

WOMAN   I think they call that a "fine line."

GARY   Hey, speaking of dark, do you like chocolate?

WOMAN   I *love* chocolate!

(Gary climbs onto a chair and grabs
a round metal container from the top
shelf in a kitchen cabinet. He turns
and shows it to Woman.)

GARY   I got nine different kinds: Milk chocolate, dark chocolate, extra-dark chocolate, chocolate with almonds, chocolate with caramel, chocolate with cherries, chocolate with raspberries, chocolate with sea salt, and chocolate with bacon.

WOMAN   *Bacon?* Are you kidding me? I'll go with the bacon! If it's free-range.

GARY   Of course it's free-range. Where do you think you're living? This is Oregon, not Texas.

(Lights out.)

Scene 3

The house.

A vase of roses, a candle, and two champagne glasses are on the dining table. Woman is sitting. Gary pops the cork on a bottle of champagne at the sink, brings the bottle over, and fills the two glasses. He lights the candle, sits at the table, and raises his glass.

GARY   I want to propose a toast.

WOMAN   A toast.

GARY   Yes.

WOMAN   What's the occasion?

GARY   Us.

WOMAN   We're the occasion?

(Woman has not picked up her glass. Gary reaches out and guides her hand to the glass. She grasps it. Gary raises her hand

and the glass. When he lets go, her hand
drops a little, not much, but enough that
Gary notices. He reaches out and takes
Woman's hand again, raising her glass to
the same level as his, correcting and con-
trolling her. This time, she keeps it there.)

GARY   I propose a toast to two people that have been
together for the entire beautiful month of October. A
man and a woman that fit together like Legos. That
stick like glue. We should be together forever, baby.

(Gary pulls a ring from his pocket
and puts it on Woman's finger.)

GARY   Will you marry me?

WOMAN   Oh my God!

(Woman looks at the ring and chugs
the entire glass of champagne.)

GARY   Is that a yes?

WOMAN   A month, Gary. You said it yourself. We've
been seeing each other for a *month*. Don't you want
to get to know me better?

GARY   No.

(A look from Woman.)

GARY   I mean, yeah, sure. But let's get married first, go
down to the courthouse tomorrow, and then we'll
start. We'll get started on knowing each other better
than anybody has ever known us.

(Woman's intuition kicks in, freezing
her power of speech.)

GARY   Come on. Whattaya say?

WOMAN   I say … tell me something about yourself.

GARY   Why?

WOMAN   Let's start right now. Tell me something that nobody knows about you.

GARY   Don't you think we should have a little mystery? Things to discover as we go?

WOMAN   Come on. It doesn't have to be big.

GARY   I already told you the big thing.

WOMAN   Then how about something smaller?

GARY   Well … sometimes I'm kind of a perfectionist.

WOMAN   Isn't that a little like saying in a job interview, "My biggest fault is that I work too hard"?

GARY   OK, how about this: I'm a nice guy.

WOMAN   A nice guy? It's a little suspicious that nobody knows that about you.

GARY   No, no, I didn't mean it like that.

WOMAN   You mean you're *not* a nice guy?

GARY   No, no, noooooo! You're twisting my words. I mean, yes, I am a nice guy. But I guess everybody already knows that about me.

WOMAN   Do you have official references on that? Are there real, living people who would confirm it?

GARY   Whew! You're hard-core. No, I do not have any signed or notarized paperwork, but there *are* people that would say that about me.

WOMAN   Everybody's got secrets. Tell me one of yours.

GARY   A secret.

WOMAN   A dark one. Like chocolate. The darker the better.

GARY   I have to think about it.

WOMAN   Think about it? Come on! The kind of secrets I'm talking about never leave the frontal lobe of your brain. They're just bouncing around, fizzing like soda pop, waiting to erupt — like herpes — at the absolute worst possible time, like, say, on the wedding night.

GARY   I see what you're saying.

WOMAN   Do you?

GARY   Uh … wait … I thought I did. You *are* talking about secrets, right, and not that other, uh, you know, eruption thing? Secrets are easy to tell because they're waiting to come out?

WOMAN   Yes. They're a burden. A secret burden. Something that weighs you down. That's why they say "get it off your chest." That's why they say "the truth will set you free."

GARY   The truth will set you free if it doesn't put you in prison.

WOMAN   So tell me a true secret that won't put you in prison.

GARY   Let's see … I guess I don't really have any secrets.

(Woman laughs loudly.)

GARY   What?

WOMAN   *Everybody* has secrets. If we went around telling people who we really are, deep down inside, the things we think, the things we want to do, the things we need to do, the things we've *done* … So everybody lies. And I do mean *everybody*. Maybe a lot of it is little stuff, but if we told the whole nothing-left-out truth, society would break down. There wouldn't *be* any society. You couldn't have a girlfriend or a boyfriend or a wife or a husband because it would be too scary. Why do you think women become nuns and men become priests?

GARY   I don't know. The whole no-sex thing, I've wondered about that.

WOMAN   Because relationships are such a big risk. Except with God. You assume he's merciful, that he's not going to hurt you … That's what they tell you, that's what they want you to believe, but come on, we both know he can ignore you when you need him the most. From what I've seen, he's mostly leading us on. He doesn't answer that many prayers.

GARY   He's overworked just like the rest of us.

WOMAN   And priests. Jesus! If the priests confessed their secrets to the nuns, those girls would go into a different line of work.

GARY   Like what? Where do you go if the church is too weird?

WOMAN   That's just it. There's no place to hide.

GARY   Except inside your own head.

WOMAN   Hmmm … that's a freaky-Freudy thing to say. Where did *that* come from?

GARY   I don't know. It just came out.

WOMAN   It sounds suspiciously like the truth. The truth has a way of just coming out.

GARY Look, are you gonna marry me? Or are we just gonna sit here all night talking about priests and nuns … I mean, if you don't want to —

WOMAN I didn't say I don't want to. But a month … that's jumping into it.

GARY You think that's fast?

WOMAN I think it's supersonic.

GARY We had sex the second time we went out.

WOMAN What took us so long?

GARY We had to wait. You were passed out on our first "date." *(He makes air quotes with his fingers)*

WOMAN Gary Smith, you might be the last gentleman left on planet Earth. OK, I'm going to tell you a secret. I'll show you how it's done. If we *had* had blackout "sex" *(she uses air quotes)* on our first "date," *(air quotes again)* I'm pretty sure it would *not* have been the first time that ever happened to me … I've never told anybody that. *That* is a secret. A big, personal one.

    (A beat as Gary considers his secrets.)

GARY I stole money out of my mother's purse one time.

WOMAN I've done that.

GARY You have?

WOMAN Sure, hasn't everybody?

GARY Actually, it was several times.

WOMAN Me, too.

    (A beat.)

GARY   And I bought drugs with it.

WOMAN   I can relate … You're pretty good at telling secrets. I'm impressed.

GARY   It's a little easier when you're telling them to someone you know, instead of your mother. Or a cop.

WOMAN   A cop?

GARY   That's just a hyperthreatical case. *(he means "hypothetical")*

WOMAN   Why does it feel so true?

GARY   Maybe you're impersonating it.

>   (Woman laughs. Rightly or wrongly, Gary senses derision, though he would not know the word. He grabs Woman's arm to make her stop.)

WOMAN   Owwwwww!

>   (Woman yanks; Gary lets go.)

GARY   Sorry.

WOMAN   What was that for?

>   (A shrug from Gary.)

WOMAN   You really know how to make a woman want to marry you.

GARY   I'm very sorry. I apologize. I took it the wrong way.

WOMAN   It?

GARY   You laughed at me. Listen: I *love* you.

>   (Woman's mouth falls open; she is unable to speak.)

GARY I love you really *big*. I *get* you. I seriously big-time want to *marry* you ... Sometimes, when I want something so bad ... so much ... I overreact. But the way I feel about you ... I feel like we could fly through the sky together. We're so much alike. We're two birds. We're two *comets*. It feels like forever.

(A beat, then Woman takes Gary's head in her hands and kisses him passionately.)

GARY Is *that* a yes?

WOMAN How would this work? Do you know how this works? Is there a lot of legal stuff to do? Doesn't it change everything?

GARY You ask a lot of questions.

WOMAN I *have* a lot of questions. Marriage scares me. I never thought I would get married. Have you ever been married? Doesn't it scare you?

GARY Woman, you sure do ask a lot of questions.

WOMAN Marriage is a big deal, Gary.

GARY I guess so.

WOMAN You *guess* so?

GARY I mean, yeah, it is. Of course it is. It's a sacred bond between two people that love each other. You do love me, don't you?

WOMAN I feel like I do ... for sure, I'm all fluttery inside ... OK, I feel like I'm a little flipped out. I said marriage scares me, but really it's more like it *terrifies* me. I feel like I don't know if that's a good sign or a bad sign. I feel like I love you as much as anybody can love somebody they've known for a month ... I feel like I might throw up.

GARY   You sure have a lot of feelings. Do ya ever feel like maybe you have too many feelings? And if you're gonna puke, do it in the bathroom. *(He points to the bedroom doorway)*

WOMAN   You just asked me to *marry* you! Aren't you supposed to have a lot of feelings?

GARY   Yeah. Sure.

WOMAN   Is this ... would this be your first time? Have you been married before?

GARY   Yeah.

WOMAN   You have?

GARY   Does that surprise you? Do I seem like the kind of guy that couldn't get someone to marry him?

WOMAN   No, not at all, I didn't mean it like that ... But ... you haven't mentioned it ... It seems like that's something —

GARY   What am I? On trial here? Do I have to bring up every little thing about my past? Do you have to know every little detail about my life? She died, OK? My wife died.

WOMAN   I'm ... that's awful ... I'm sorry.

GARY   Are you happy now?

WOMAN   No.

GARY   And in case you were wondering, which you probably were, she died in a car crash. Speeding. OK? Does that satisfy your curiosity?

WOMAN   Gary, please, I'm sorry. I didn't mean to upset you.

GARY   I don't need this kind of stress in my life. I've got enough as it is.

(Gary gets up, crosses the room
to a cabinet, and opens it.)

GARY   You want to be all curious like a cat?

(Gary pulls a meth pipe out
of the cabinet.)

GARY   You want to ask questions about every little
thing?

(Gary returns to the table.)

GARY   You want to know a secret?

(Gary pushes the vase of roses aside
and sets the meth pipe down on the
table in front of Woman.)

GARY   Ask me about this.

(Woman takes a long look at the
pipe and then a long look at Gary.
She caresses the pipe, which is
beautiful, a work of glass art.)

(Gary expects Woman to walk out
— but she doesn't. She continues
admiring the pipe. She picks up
the burning candle with her free
hand and holds it next to the pipe.)

WOMAN   I've only got one question: Are we going to
fire this thing up, or are we just going to sit here all
night talking about marriage?

(Lights out.)

Scene 4

The house.

The front door flies open. Exuberantly happy, Gary carries Woman inside, whirling her around, dipping, waltzing. They both have wedding rings. Woman is wearing a tattered white dress from a thrift store.

GARY I'm going to carry you across this threshold every day for the rest of our lives! … Now, for the after-party. Where to put you down?

WOMAN *(drunkenly singing)* Ohhh, nooooo … don't put me dooownnn … ohhh, nooooo, puh-leeaaze, don't put me dooownnn … Don't you ever … ever … *ever* … *EVER* … put me, put me, put me *(she is howling now)* dooow ooow ooow ooowwwnnnnn!

GARY Catchy tune. You could be a backup singer for wolves. All right, let's think about this … The marriage bed? … No, too predictable.

WOMAN You're too *delectable!*

GARY The Lazy Boy? No. Been there, broke that … The floor?

WOMAN No! Splinters.

GARY By the fireplace?

WOMAN Too hot!

GARY By the fridge?

WOMAN Too cold!

(Lights begin a slow fade.)

GARY How about the table?

WOMAN Just right!

> (The vase of roses still sits atop the dining
> table. Gary swings Woman's legs so they
> knock the vase out of the way. It crashes to
> the floor. He lowers her onto the table, on
> her back. Woman spreads her legs, point-
> ing them toward the sky, a V shape. She
> holds her arms up in a V shape. She makes
> a V with the fingers of both hands. There
> are four V's facing downstage: Her legs,
> arms, and fingers of both hands.)

WOMAN *(sexy)* Knock, knooooooccckkkkk.

GARY Who's there?

WOMAN Piece.

> (A beat as Gary takes in the view.)

GARY I *love* marriage!

WOMAN I love *you!*

> (Blackout.)

Scene 5

The house.

Gary and Woman are lovey-dovey on the couch downstage. Gary is sitting up, and Woman is lying down
with her head in his lap, looking up at his face.

GARY Do you believe in love at first sight?

WOMAN   Not really. My vision is terrible.

GARY   I do.

WOMAN   I don't know. Maybe it happens. But only in the movies. I like old movies, though, even if they're not realistic. There's something about riding off into a golden sunset.

GARY   It happened to me.

WOMAN   Seriously?

GARY   Very seriously.

WOMAN   Did it work out? I've never heard of love at first sight working out. I've never seen any evidence that it works out. Maybe with rose-colored 3D glasses at the Imax. Maybe love reaches out and slaps you in the face.

GARY   Oh, it worked out all right. You and me. We were destiny.

WOMAN   Huh?

GARY   You and me. It was love at first sight.

WOMAN   *We* were love at first sight?

GARY   I had fireworks in my heart. It was like the Fourth of July and Halloween and Christmas and Independence Day all rolled into one.

WOMAN   I think I would remember that. I *should* remember that. So there were … explosions?

GARY   Damn right. My heart exploded like an M-80 wrapped in bottle rockets with sparklers on top. My head, too. I'm lucky to be alive.

WOMAN   Where was this?

GARY   In Old Town. On Second Avenue.

WOMAN Oh, right, our first "date." *(air quotes)* … I don't exactly remember it.

GARY Nothing like a good fade-to-black.

WOMAN Kind of a real-life movie, I guess. Gone with the Binge.

GARY I picked you up … out of a puddle of vomit.

WOMAN Was it mine?

GARY I hope so. It took me a long time to get you cleaned up.

WOMAN Now that is romantic. *That* should be a movie.

GARY The lighting isn't too bad in Old Town. It's a warm light. Kind of orange. A good orange, though, not like candy corn. That light can tell a story.

WOMAN I sort of remember a lot of dark places. Most of those lights are burned out.

GARY They get replaced. If you're near a corner, you always get a little glow.

WOMAN No doubt, everybody hanging out around there is lit up.

GARY You don't remember me carrying you to the waterfront? Talk about a movie. It was very movie-like. Like a Spielburger film. With extra cheese.

WOMAN So I was in a movie? *Our* movie?

GARY You really don't remember that night?

WOMAN Was I at least semi-conscious at some point? Did my eyelashes flutter? Did I say anything?

GARY You came to … after a while. I think you understood that something cine-magical was going on. We introduced ourselves. I got your number. The evening was warm. There was chemistry. Elements were combining.

(Woman reaches up and caresses Gary's stubbly cheek.)

WOMAN   You're a knight in shining Technicolor armor.

GARY   Ha! There *was* a horse involved. You remember that?

WOMAN   Maybe. I'm getting that vague dream feeling.

GARY   A cop came by — on a horse. I guess it looked weird. We were soaking wet. I was washing your hair in the Skidmore Fountain.

WOMAN   So it was an Italian movie.

GARY   At first I thought he was rousting us, but then I saw the subtitles.

WOMAN   The cop was subtitled?

GARY   It's the only way I could understand him.

WOMAN   What did he say?

GARY   *(Italian accent)*   You two a-belong-a-together. Have a-good-a-night.

WOMAN   The subtitles had an accent?

GARY   It made sense to me at the time.

WOMAN   Do you want to make Italian movie love to me?

GARY   Always and forever. Italian *and* French. You wanna get high first?

WOMAN   Oh, yeah, foreplay! Then you can carry me over to the waterfront. Let's do it there. For old times' sake. Let's make some memories I can remember.

GARY   I'd like that.

WOMAN   Four Loins in the Fountain.

> (Gary reaches over Woman and grasps
> a meth pipe off the normal coffee table.)

GARY   Would m'lady mind holding our matrimethical pipe for a little minute?   *(he probably means "matrimonial")*

> (Woman offers Gary her open hand, and he
> places the pipe into it. He reaches for a can-
> dle on the table. He pulls a lighter from his
> pocket and lights the candle, then places it
> back on the table. He returns the lighter to
> his pants pocket. Gary pulls a foil of meth
> from his shirt pocket. Woman sits up and
> holds the pipe in position so Gary can fill it.
> They work well together, a well-oiled duo.)

> (After he empties the meth into the pipe,
> Gary crumples up the foil and tosses it over
> his shoulder onto the floor, with no regard
> for where it lands.)

> (He reaches for the candle and holds it un-
> der the pipe, which he offers to Woman.
> She takes the first hit.)

> (Lights fade. The only illumination seems
> to be the candle.)

> (Gary takes a hit off the pipe. He places it
> on the table. He continues to hold the can-
> dle, using it to illuminate Woman's face.
> They stare into each other's eyes, and then
> they kiss, tenderly. If they weren't smoking
> meth, it might be romantic. But it's difficult

to tell which they love more, each other
or the extremely dangerous drug.)

(Gary blows out the candle.)

(Blackout.)

Scene 6

The house.

Gary is sacked out on the couch, drinking beer, watching mindless TV, channel surfing with the remote control. Woman enters, home from work. She heads for the kitchen and busies herself. Gary doesn't look at her.

GARY *(he clicks the remote to change channels)* Hey, baby-maybe.

WOMAN Hi.

GARY What time is it? What are you doing home? What's going on?

WOMAN Nothing.

GARY It doesn't sound like nothing. *(clicks the remote)* It's not even noon yet. Is it?

WOMAN I'm sorry, Gary.

GARY For what?

WOMAN Please don't be mad, OK?

(Now Gary pays attention. He clicks off the television and turns toward Woman.)

GARY Tell me what I shouldn't be mad about.

WOMAN I lost my job.

GARY   Lost it. You mean it's going to China? Or India? Or Pakighanistan? Or … where do they send our jobs nowadays, anyway?

WOMAN   No. I got fired.

GARY   What happened?

WOMAN   They made us take a urine test.

GARY   That's a real pisser.

   (Quick beat. They laugh at the same time. The tension is broken.)

GARY   So an insurance company is worried about whether you get high? Seems like they wouldn't mind. Don't you lose more claims when you're cruising at 35,000 feet?

WOMAN   Are you mad?

GARY   Do I look mad?

WOMAN   No.

GARY   Do you know how many jobs I've been fired from in my life?

WOMAN   No.

GARY   You know how the eskimos have a hundred different words for snow?

WOMAN   Yeah.

GARY   They've got a hundred and fifty words for ways that I've been canned.

WOMAN   That sounds like a lot.

GARY   I've been canned more times than albacore tuna. I lost my first job when I was 10 years old. I had a paper route.

WOMAN   They fire 10-year-old kids?

GARY   Here's a secret for you: This old lady refused to pay me after I rode in her yard, so I tossed my bicycle through her living room window.

(A beat as Woman registers
this information.)

WOMAN   Gary, I will get another job. I will clean up and find something.

GARY   Don't worry about it.

WOMAN   What do you mean?

GARY   Don't get another job.

WOMAN   What about the money? I got fired. I won't get unemployment.

GARY   You were making ten twenty-five an hour. Why bother trying to get another nowhere job like that? Forget it. I'll put in some overtime, work a few side angles with people I know. We'll sell some stuff. We'll be OK. I love you. That's the only thing that matters. I am going to take care of you.

(A beat as Woman gets emotional.)

WOMAN   I don't know what to say. I love you, too. Nobody has ever done anything like that for me … You're going to make me cry.

GARY   *(arms open wide)*   Come here.

(Wiping away a tear, Woman
goes to Gary. They embrace.)

(Lights fade out.)

Scene 7

The house.

Woman is a mess, all sprawled out on the floor. Gary is cooking something on the stove in a frying pan.

GARY Wake up, Woman. It's time for lunch. *(sing-song)* I'm making a raspberry jello omm-uhh-lette.

> (No response from Woman. Gary walks over and shoves her with his foot. She freaks out, as if disoriented and awaking from a nightmare. She frantically slaps and picks at imaginary insects on her skin as Gary walks back to the stove.)

GARY I said, I'm making a RASPBERRY JELLO OMELETTE!

WOMAN *(foggy)* Raspberry? … Omelette? … Will you feed it to me?

GARY You smell like wet dog. We don't have any spoons.

> (Woman tries to get up; she makes it to her knees but collapses back to the floor. She lies there, trying to gather enough strength to rise.)

WOMAN Have we got any forks?

GARY No, none of that stuff … silverware. We don't have any silverware. No goldware, either.

WOMAN Didn't we used to have some?

GARY What did you do, pawn it? Those were my grandma's coke spoons … But I wouldn't exactly call silverware a necessary. *(he means "necessity")* People survived before they invented forks. I'd rather have fire than forks. I'd rather have *food* than forks.

(Gary puts on an old oven mitt and carries the frying pan over to Woman. He offers her a handful of omelette. She gets on her hands and knees and takes a bite.)

WOMAN *(like a crazy Pomeranian dog)* Woof! Arrf! Yip! Yap! Yip! Yip! Grrffff!

GARY Don't be a bitch.

WOMAN That means I like it.

GARY You did some howling last night. Off the leash!

WOMAN What's in this? It's really good.

GARY Raspberry jello and eggs.

WOMAN Do they still make raspberry jello?

GARY I don't know. It might be seasonal. I got it at work. Somebody left it in the ink closet.

(Gary takes a bite, eating with his hand.)

WOMAN Is this your own recipe?

GARY Yeah, six eggs and a box of jello. The key is to mix well, then cook the eggs perfectly.

WOMAN It makes me pucker up. There's a big, sweet buzz to it. What do you call that?

GARY Tartsy-fartsy.

(Gary feeds her another mouthful. He takes a bite, too, licks off his fingers.)

WOMAN   Right, tart. *(sings like Janis Joplin)* Take it, take another little piece-a-my tart now, baby!

GARY   I wonder if I could get a part-time job in a restaurant. I can cook. They must always need cooks. Or I could fix flat tires on food carts. Maybe that's an up-and-coming job. That would be working in the food industry. Start there. Get a foot in the door. I could make those bomb-me sandwiches. *(he means "banh mi")* Can't be that hard. Bring in some extra money. I wonder how much those guys get paid. Better be more than minimum wage. I dunno. It's probably boring. And they probably pay you in sandwiches.

WOMAN   They say that in the new "land-on-your-feet" economy, we're going to have to reinvent ourselves nine times during our lives. Like a cat.

GARY   What they really mean is, you're going to have to *die* nine times. Anyway, who's "they"? *They* probably never had a real job. *They* probably just sit around all day scamming money off people that do actual work.

WOMAN   I think you're talking about Wall Street bankers.

GARY   Yeah, if it wasn't for them, we'd be doing OK. If Wall Street bankers want to make a real contribution to society, they should go fuck themselves for 40 hours a week.

WOMAN   They say we're all going to be replaced by robots anyway.

GARY   I'd like to see a robot ink a seven-color flaming skull on the jiggly ass of a 300-pound biker chick from Idaho.

WOMAN *(mechanical robot voice)* Beep. Boop. Fleep. Circuit overload. Need more ink. Ass exceeds capacity.

GARY *(biker chick voice)*   I think something's wrong. My ass is numb! Oh, God, I can't feel my ass! *(Gary's real voice)* Yeah, get off the Harley for five minutes and do a few deep knee bends and some jumping jacks.

WOMAN   People don't take care of themselves anymore.

> (Lights out.)

Scene 8

The house.

Frantic and occasionally incoherent, Woman is whirling around the room, twitching, groaning, shrieking, slapping her arms and legs, scratching at phantom insects that are crawling under her skin.

WOMAN   Aaaiiieeeee … *Oww!* No! Stop, please! *Stop it!* Leave me alone! Don't fush mish! Dirty bloosh, darfuss dirt of the soul. Goaf! I'm not coming bash! Villful liffus raggus alsh.

> (Woman spies something on the table that only she can see. She puts her finger to her lips to tell everybody to be quiet.)

WOMAN   Shhhhhhh …

> (Woman sneaks up on the apparition. Realizing she needs a weapon to kill her prey,

Woman turns to a cabinet and grabs a
dinner plate. She returns to stalking the
prey, slowly, stealthily. Then she strikes,
smashing the plate onto the table top.)

WOMAN   Die, motherbugger!

(Pieces of plate go flying. Gary, who has
crashed on the floor near the table, awak-
ens to the mayhem. Moving as if in pain,
he brushes shards off his clothing.)

GARY   What the? *Hey!*

WOMAN   Get off! Get off me!

(Gary manages to get on his feet. He goes
after the crazed Woman. She fights him off
as if he is one of the unseen bugs invading
her. He slaps her in the face. He spins her
around and wraps his arms around her. She
writhes and screams. Gary puts one hand
over Woman's mouth to stop the noise.)

GARY   Shut up! Shut your mouth! … You know, the
bugs only burrow into the skin of loudmouth paranoid freak-out people. The bugs *love* noise. It's like
food to them. They want to sink their teeth into it.

(Woman calms down.)

GARY   OK, good, that's better. Now if I let you go, are
you gonna chill? 'Cause if you're not, I'm gonna tie
you up with duct tape and throw you in the basement
with all the spiders. So don't make me do that. Just
don't! Understand?

(Woman nods meekly. Gary is leery, but he
slowly begins to disengage. When he lets

go of Woman, she flips out again, worse
than before, shrieking and spouting nonsense as the unseen insects ravage her.)

(She runs across the room, grabs a painting
off the wall, and begins swatting at phan-
tasms. Gary grabs a glass from the kitchen
and throws it at her. The glass shatters on
the wall.)

(Blackout.)

Scene 9

The house.

Woman is in the kitchen, cooking scrambled eggs. Gary
enters from the bedroom, hung over, looking slovenly.

WOMAN   Good morning.

> (Gary holds up his hand, a signal
> to Woman to stop talking.)

GARY   We'll see.

> (In a royal funk, Gary sits down at
> the table like a king, expecting that
> breakfast will be served to him.)

WOMAN   I'm making eggs. I got some plastic sporks.

GARY   Maybe there will be a time in our lives for mean-
ingless jabbering about sporks, but this is not it. Forget about sporks. Sporks are for people with no con-
victions. There's a steak knife in the drawer. Give me
that. Nothing says "I love you" like a knife.

(Woman silently finishes cooking the eggs and puts them on a plate. She sets the plate and the steak knife carefully on the table in front of Gary. He touches the plate.)

GARY   This plate is cold.

WOMAN   I'll warm it up for you.

(Gary holds up his hand, a stop sign.)

GARY   Maybe that won't be necessary.

(Wielding the knife blade like a spoon, Gary takes a bite of the eggs. He spits them out, smashes the plate on the floor, and stabs the steak knife into the table top. The blade goes clear through; the knife is in *deep*.)

GARY   The eggs are overcooked.

(Woman stoops and grabs the biggest piece of shattered plate. She rises and starts to pull the knife out of the table.)

GARY   NO! Don't touch that knife! *Not ever!*

(Gary shoves away from the table and motions to his lap.)

GARY   Come here. Sit.

(Woman sits. Gary grabs the broken piece of plate out of her hand and throws it on the floor.)

GARY   You know I love you, don't you?

(Woman shakes her head yes, but it's barely perceptible.)

GARY OK. Good. If nothing else, we will always have that. That is the bond between us. Nobody can ever take that away. The thing is, there are certain rules. We have to have certain *rules*. Now you know how I like my eggs, because —

WOMAN Not overcoo —

(Gary slaps Woman's face.)

GARY *(calmly)* Let me finish. You know how I like my eggs, because I have told you this before. Several times. I don't ask much of you. In fact, I should ask a lot more. But I don't want to pile too much on your plate. However, the one thing that I have told you before is the one thing that is very important to me. Something that you must get right. Scrambled eggs should be cooked just beyond runny, but not solid, not dry. You stir them with a wooden spatula, you keep stirring them. As they firm up, you get ready to turn off the flame. Your number one job is to turn off the flame about thirty seconds before they're done, so they cook for a few final moments on the heat of the frying pan. When they get to slightly moist and fluffy, you're finished. You have cooked the perfect eggs. Do you understand? Because I don't want to have to tell you this one important thing again.

(Woman nods yes.)

GARY Don't just nod. Speak! DO ... YOU ... UNDER ... STAND?

WOMAN Yes.

GARY OK. Good. Now let's try it again.

(Woman rises and goes to the stove.)

GARY Aren't you going to clean up your mess first?

WOMAN I'm sorry. Yes.

GARY A clean kitchen is the sign of an orderly, disciplined mind. God knows, you could use two or three shots of discipline.

   (Lights out.)

Scene 10

In the dark, the sound of a thunderclap. It is raining. We hear water dripping onto steel surfaces.

Lights up on the house.

Buckets and pans are spread around on the floor to catch drops of water leaking through the roof.

Gary is sitting at the dining table, cleaning a meth pipe. Woman is washing a big pot in the sink.

WOMAN Why does it have to rain so much? I *hate* the rain.

GARY Is that pot for dinner or the leak?

WOMAN The leak.

GARY Why are you washing it?

WOMAN It's filthy.

GARY Use your brain, Woman. You're going to set it under running water. Nature's dishwasher.

   (Woman quits washing the pot
   and carries it to the last leak that
   does not have a bucket under it,
   downstage center. She looks up

and watches the water. She puts
the pot on top of her head, then
steps under the leak. Drip, drip.)

WOMAN I'm moving to Africa.

GARY No you're not.

WOMAN Where the sun shines all the time. Where it's
warm.

GARY You wanna carry water ten miles to your mud
hut? Into each woman's life a few raindrops must keep
fallin' upon her weary head.

WOMAN Not in Africa.

GARY Africa's a big country. I guarantee you there's
ten thousand women over there right now sayin', "I'm
moving to cold, gray, rainy, moldy, foggy Portland."

WOMAN I'll trade places with them.

GARY You need to get back to reality. You need to get
high.

WOMAN I need to get lost. In *Africa.*

GARY I understand that smoking rhino horn makes
you feel like you're the lion king of the jungle.

(Woman takes the pot off of her
head and places it on the floor,
under the leak. Drip, drip, drip.)

WOMAN We've got to fix the roof.

GARY Why?

WOMAN Because it's leaking.

GARY It'll quit leaking as soon as the rain stops. In
ten minutes, max. It can't rain really hard like this
for more than ten minutes.

WOMAN   What if it doesn't stop? What if it rains like this for forty days and forty nights?

GARY   We'll build an ark. We'll load it up with male and female marijuana plants, sail to Africa, and pick up some zig-zags.

WOMAN   Zig-zags?

GARY   They're all over the jungle, running away from the lions.

WOMAN   You mean zebras.

GARY   Yeah, zebras. That's what I said.

WOMAN   An ark … that's getting back to reality.

GARY   Reality is boring. Reality will kill you. Right after it kills your dreams. If you have any.

WOMAN   Damn. I do need to get high.

GARY   See? I told you. Woman needs to get high. All right! Come fly with me.

>   (Woman joins Gary at the table. They
>   each take a hit off the meth pipe. Then
>   Gary gets up, energized and enthused.)

GARY   Dance with me.

WOMAN   Huh?

GARY   *Dance with me!* I'll be Fred Astaire and you be Roy Rogers.

WOMAN   You mean Ginger Rogers.

GARY   Whatever. Just dance with me.

WOMAN   *(motions to the dripping rain)*   Look at this place. You should be Gene Kelly.

GARY Fine. I'm Keen Jelly. Come on! Get up! Dance with me! Let's twickle the ivories with our tinkle toes.

WOMAN Do you think dancing under the influence is a good idea? We'll probably slip and fall and break our necks. You won't be tickling your toes when you get paralyzed from the neck down.

GARY See? That's reality talking. Screw reality. If we get paralyzed, we'll stop dancing. OK? Does that make you feel better?

WOMAN Not really.

> (Gary starts doing a silly, funktastic
> dance, whirling around the living room,
> weaving in between the pots and pans
> on the floor. As he boogies and struts,
> he chants like an African tribesman.)

GARY Uooogga booogga, bamma lamma, whoompa shoompa, snooga wooga, raga daga, machu picchu, the lion ain't sleepin' tonight, baby-maybe! Dooga deega, gotsu geetsu, oooeeee ooowaaaa, NO RAIN! Luueee loowow, riffa whiffa, dansa wansa, NO RAIN! Oommm babba, zooom babba, oommm babba wabba babba, oommm babba, baby wamma, oommm babba, baby wamma, NO RAIN! NO RAIN! Oommm babba, baby zomma, NOOOOOOOOOOO RAIN!

> (Occasionally, Woman joins in with
> some gibberish of her own, mimick-
> ing Gary, or maybe mocking him.)

WOMAN Lava wava, chockla cheekla, twitchin witchin, cows in the kitchen, NOOOOO RAIN! Fava beano, weeno wino, saba suba, tuba wooba, dancy wancy, antsy pantsy, keefer weefer, NOOOO RAIN! ... NO RAIN! NO RAIN! NOOOOOOO RAIN!

(Gary jumps up on a chair, his arms reach-
ing for heaven. He feels the spirit, as if in a
Pentecostal trance with a full summer sun
shining down upon his inner wild child. His
African chanting changes momentarily to
gibberish, a sputtering speaking-in-tongues,
his own personal mystery language. Then it
mutates again, to a declaration delivered
with such power and fury that it seems to be
coming not just from him, but from the entire universe. OK, that's an exaggeration.
Nevertheless, methed-up megalomaniacal
nonsense spews from his mouth.)

GARY Ohhveeega nifloom … vasarrvia victus niktoo
… reeflavius eyeflecto … narruunda vundum ton-
nikus … deesenza ovakkatassa … differessess
vishuvvio pappallya … For I am the almighty African
sun god, Melanomus Laviticus, and I alone rule the
infinite, ceaseless sands of time, gathering them up,
dispensing them to great dunes, vast worlds of sand,
ever expanding universes of sand that swallow up the
rain, burn it, bake it, candlestick make it — and there-
fore, as is my divine right, I decree that from this gray
day forward, from this moment until the dark, everlasting end, when I dance, the rain shall stop, when I
twirl, the rain shall shrink, when I shimmy, the rain
shall shiver and shake. Vanish, oh buzzkill bummer
rain, be gone when I dance.

(Gary puts one foot up on the back of the
chair, and tips it over, just like Fred Astaire
would. He rides the chair down to the
floor, landing on his feet, and begins to
dance, dance, dance, with crazy drug-

fueled abandon, arms akimbo, arms aloft,
arms flailing, torso twisting, feet flying.)

GARY   Oh, rain, we do not love you anymore, it is not
you, it is us. Be gone, be gone, be gone, and do not —
do not — come back. Desert us now, for we long for
the desert.

>   (Gary grabs one of the pans on the floor and
>   flings it into the air. The water sprays. He
>   catches the pan on the way down and begins
>   to use it as a tambourine, beating out a vivid
>   rhythm. He steps onto one of the chairs at
>   the dining table and leaps onto the table top,
>   where he continues to dance, dance, dance,
>   some Michael Jackson-meets-Masai-warrior
>   moves. Woman grabs the meth pipe off the
>   table — protectively — and retreats to
>   safer ground.)

>   (**Note:** The steak knife is still stuck in the
>   table top and will remain there until Scene
>   17. Gary dances around it.)

GARY   *(moving to the tambourine beat)*   Oom booga
looga wooga, oom booga looga wooga, bam wamma
tamma lamma, bam wamma tamma lamma —
NOOOOO RAIN! Oom booga looga wooga, oom
booga looga wooga, bam wamma tamma lamma, bam
wamma tamma lamma, NOOOO RAIN! NO RAIN!
NO RAIN! NO RAIN! NO RAIN! NOOOOOOO-
OOOOOOOOOOOO RAAAAAAAAAIIIIIIIINN!

>   (One table leg breaks; the table tips over.
>   Gary plunges to the floor, not at all like
>   Fred Astaire. He lands in a heap, dazed.)

WOMAN   Oh my God!

(She rushes to Gary's side.)

WOMAN Is your neck all right?

(Gary moves cautiously, checking himself over. He wiggles both feet, swivels his neck and hands. Everything seems to be in place. He raises his arm and points to the ceiling.)

GARY See?

WOMAN Your arm — is it OK?

GARY It stopped raining.

(Woman gazes at the ceiling, and around the room at the buckets. She looks back at Gary. Indeed, the rain has stopped.)

WOMAN Wow!

GARY *(Narcissistic)* The magic that is Gary.

WOMAN I thought you were Melanomus Laviticus.

GARY *(charming)* One and the same. And I, Gary Melanomus Laviticus Smith, request the pleasure of your company in a dance to bring back the sun.

(Gary holds out his hand. Woman is reluctant, but she does give him her hand, and they begin to dance, to the music they hear in their heads, apparently different tunes, so it's awkward at first, but they get better as they go. As their steps begin to synchronize, the lights go down, except for one, a golden spot — the "sun" — shining from the back of the theater. Soon they are dancing and prancing in ecstatic unison, and the warm spotlight follows them around the stage. Then ...)

(Blackout.)

(Ten seconds go by in the dark, in silence, and nothing happens.)

(Are we going to intermission? Have the house lights failed? No, this is just a little suspension, an unsettling scene change that will illustrate the vast range of Gary's instant mood swings. But what triggers his outbursts? It doesn't matter. It could be anything that Woman has done, the wrong word, the wrong look, imperfect cooking, failure to submit, a ride home, a phone call from a friend, the way she exhales, and on and on.)

(From out of the darkness, searing flashes of lightning illuminate the stage. We hear several blasts of thunder. Then, from Woman, comes a terrible scream.)

(Suddenly the stage is blasted by a powerful strobe light as …)

(Gary punches Woman in the stomach.)

(She staggers; she doubles over.)

(Gary pushes her, and she tumbles onto the normal coffee table. It collapses.)

(Woman falls to the floor.)

(The strobe light renders Gary's mystifying, tripwire rage in staccato bursts of violence.)

GARY YOU STUPID SLUT WHORE, YOU NEVER
DO THAT AGAIN, DO YOU HEAR ME? *NEVER!*
YOU EVER DO THAT AGAIN, I WILL KILL YOU.
I WILL STAB YOU IN YOUR UGLY FUCKING
FACE!

(Gary grabs a kitchen chair and throws it
across the room. He rushes to the front
door, flings it open, and storms out of the
house. He does not bother to shut the door
— he must get away from Woman, or he
might kill her right now.)

(A thunderclap punctuates Gary's exit.)

(The strobe light continues to flash upon
this tableau of intimidation and fury.)

(Blackout.)

(One more blast of lightning and thunder.)

(Another ten seconds of silence go by in the
dark.)

(Now the house lights come up, and we go
to intermission.)

(**Note on a set change:** The normal, now-
smashed coffee table is replaced with the
door-on-blocks "coffee table" from Scene 1,
for the duration of the play.)

Act II

Scene 11

A hospital bed.

Lights up on Woman in the hospital bed. We hear footsteps echoing offstage. They get louder and louder. The footsteps stop, and Gary sticks his head into the room, tentatively. He sees Woman, then enters. He approaches the bed.

GARY Hey, baby-maybe … It's me … How are you feeling? … Can you hear me?

(Haggard and out of it, Woman moans.)

GARY You look good.

WOMAN Gary?

GARY Yeah, it's me. I came to see you. I came to see if you need anything. How are you doing?

WOMAN My arm hurts.

GARY You had a pretty bad fall … so … your arm hurts?

WOMAN Yes.

GARY Let me take a look.

(Gary pulls down the sheet.
Woman's arm is in a cast.)

GARY Whoa! … They gave you a cast? … For that?

WOMAN It's broken. It hurts.

GARY Really … They said it's broken? Funny. They didn't tell me that. Don't worry. I straightened stuff up at home. I organized all day and all night. Moved some furniture. It's easy to trip on things, you know? Nasty fall you took.

(No response from Woman.)

GARY Listen. Are we good? I came to take you home. Things are cool at home now. No more tripping hazards. I took care of everything. It's all baby-proof. It's all baby-*maybe*-proof. So it's time to come home.

WOMAN I don't think so. I think I better stay here. I don't … I don't feel so good.

GARY This is a hospital. Nobody feels good. But you can't stay here.

WOMAN My arm hurts.

GARY Yeah, you said that five or six times. Listen, I got a plan. We'll stop smoking … We'll stop smoking *for a while*. In the meantime, I can help you with your arm. I got you a little present. Some Oxy.

WOMAN *(still hazy)* Oxy.

GARY It'll help with the pain. Even if it hurts, you won't feel it. Oxy gonna make everything all *right* all *right* all *right,* oh, *yeah!* Like nothing ever happened. Smooth and sweet. It's beautiful. It's prescription.

WOMAN From the doctor? A real doctor? You got a real prescription?

GARY Sure ... well ... basically ... but that's not important now. We'll talk about the Oxy in a minute. We got more important things to discuss ... equally important. You need to explain for the doctors how you fell — how you hurt your arm. And then they'll let you go. You can come home. You can come home today. You want to come home, don't you? I already told them, but they want to hear it from you. So, you remember, right? The coffee table is in an awkward place. You tripped over it ... Right?

WOMAN You got mad. We got into a ... I don't remember much, but I remember ... We'd been smoking. A lot. I remember that we smoked a lot.

GARY *(overlapping "we smoked a lot")* You *can't* tell them that. NO! DON'T SAY THAT!

(Gary strokes her hair, lovingly.)

GARY Listen, this is important. You know I love you, right? Nobody else does. Nobody else loves you the way I do. Nobody ever will. I am here. Now. Your husband is here for you. You don't see anybody else here now, do you? Is there anybody else here for you? Coming to take you home? I don't see anybody. Do you see anybody? Is there anybody here but me?

(Woman thinks about this.)

WOMAN No.

GARY That's right. There's nobody here for you. Nobody but me. That's the way it is. That's the way it will always be. You're my wife. Forever. Don't ever forget that.

(Gary kisses her on the forehead.)

WOMAN *(sobering realization)* Forever.

GARY   I love you so much. You're my world. You know that? You are my whole world … Now the doctor, or the nurse, or the janitor, or the somebody is going to come by and ask you some questions … like they don't have anything better to do. They want to hear from *you* how you tripped and fell and hurt your arm … which is what caused the bruises.

WOMAN   Questions?

GARY   That's right. They'll just ask you a couple of questions about how you fell. And you tell them how you tripped on the coffee table.

WOMAN   I tripped?

GARY   Goddammit! Are you *on* something? Are you *high?* What kinda crazy crap did they give you?

(Gary grabs her face and squeezes it.)

GARY   Listen to me, and listen like your life depends on it. If you're listening, if you can hear me, shake your head. Like this.

(Gary shakes Woman's head for her, as if manipulating a puppet. Then he lets go. Woman feebly shakes her head yes.)

GARY   OK, good. Now you understand that you fell, right? You tripped on that coffee table we're always banging into, right?

(Woman nods, with great effort.)

GARY   OK, good, we're cool then. Now, I've got that little present for you … Actually it's big. A big little homecoming gift. And not something stupid like a vacuum cleaner or a set of snow tires.

(Gary takes a bottle of Oxycontin pills
out of his pocket and shakes it like a
maraca. Forming a one-man conga
line, he dances around Woman's bed.
He accompanies himself with the rau-
cous rattling of the bottle of pills.)

GARY *(manic)* You know what these are? These are
little angels, with halos and harps and wings and bells,
and they are gonna fly right through your brain with a
sweet, warm, loving, everlasting *LOVE* that will melt
your heart and your eyes and your brain and your eye-
balls and your brain like dark chocolate in a saucepan.
God Baby Jesus himself is gonna come on down, yeah,
little holy baby roller, roll on down and caress this
Woman's poor broken body like Saint Rollerblade of
the Laying-On-of-Hands Massage-O-Matic Monkey.
Foxy Oxy tells the sweet, honest-to-Lord-God-Father-
Holy-Jesus-Ghost *TRUTH,* baby! Oh, yeah, you will
float away and rise up and fly with golden angel wings
on puffy, sweet, cotton-candy clouds of truth and love
and bliss and beauty and no down payment!

(Gary waits for Woman to respond.
She takes her time, trying to grasp
what this onslaught-for-Oxy means.)

WOMAN I don't know, Gary.

GARY You don't know?

WOMAN I don't know.

GARY I don't believe this! *How can you not know?*

WOMAN I don't even know how I got here. Why am I
in this bed? What happened? I don't remember. And
now I'm in a hospital with a broken arm. That kind of
scares me, you know?

GARY   There's nuthin' to be scared of. You fell. Do ya remember that I already told you that? Like about eight times. So this is the ninth time. You *fell*. You klutzed right on the coffee table. Smashed it to pieces. Ruined it. I oughta make you pay for it. But I'm not going to. You got enough problems. So we'll just call it good for now. You know what I'm sayin'?

WOMAN   I know what you told me. You told me I fell. You told me about fifteen times.

GARY   What are you sayin'? You don't believe me?

WOMAN   I'm saying, all I know is what you told me.

GARY   LISTEN! If I tell you you fell on the coffee table, THEN YOU FELL ON THE COFFEE TABLE! And that's what I'm tellin' you. Because that's what happened. That's what you need to tell the doctor. Otherwise, you're not gettin' outta here — NEITHER OF US ARE!

WOMAN   Please don't get angry.

GARY   *I'M NOT ANGRY!*

WOMAN   OK, OK.

GARY   Sorry. I should keep my voice down in here. But it really ticks me off when you tell me not to get angry. You see how that works?

WOMAN   It's kind of ironic.

GARY   Screw ironic. Ironic is for people with thick glasses, people that say stuff they don't really mean, or they mean it in a backwards way that you're not supposed to get because they think you're stupid. What kind of communication is that? They don't want you to know what they really mean? I've had enough of that in my life!

(Gary holds up an Oxycontin pill. He
moves it in close to Woman's face.)

GARY   All I'm sayin' is, give it a chance. Give this holy
little pill one chance. You wanna talk about ironic?
This broken arm is gonna be the best thing to ever
happen to you — because of this little pill. If this
thing doesn't make every pain go away, if it doesn't
float you off into a golden palace in the sky, then never
take another one. If it doesn't make every problem in
your life disappear like shazam, like magic, then never
take another one.

(Woman has to think about it.)

WOMAN   All right. I'll take one. *Only* one.

GARY   That's what I'm talkin' about! That's one of the
many reasons I love you. You *TRY* stuff. You're not
afraid.

WOMAN   Are you high right now?

GARY   Maybe a little. And I wanna keep it going.

(He puts the Oxycontin pill on his tongue
and swallows. Then he gets another one
out of the bottle and puts it on Woman's
tongue. She swallows. Gary climbs into
bed with Woman and starts to "work it"
under the covers.)

GARY   Let's get those panties off. Oxy sex is like ten
thousand dream angels blessing and caressing your
fun zones in a jacuzzi tub filled with warm chocolate
syrup and strawberry jello and whipped cream. Who
knows how much this bed is costing somebody? We
might as well use it. I'll be real careful with your arm.

(Blackout.)

Scene 12

The house.

Two points of view: For Woman, the lighting is pulsing, paranoid, hallucinatory, psychotic. Occasionally, vents in the floor erupt in steam and smoke, as if fissures in the house's foundation lead directly to hell. However, when we switch to Gary's point of view, the lighting is "normal."

The sound design: There are rumbly creaks, comatose groans, indistinct voices, echoing words, ghastly slithers, scurrying worms, zippy swipes, and digestive gurgles when we are in Woman's world.

These eerie sounds and a prerecorded male voice, the voice of Woman's father, emanate from various places, stage left, stage right, the ceiling, the back of the theater. The voice is heavily processed — rapid panning, pitch shift, modulation, delay, stutter edits, reverb — to produce a nightmare quality.

Sometimes the voice is looped. Sometimes it overlaps itself — spliced and diced, mixed and matched, loops playing at the same time to become a cacophony. When Gary enters, however, the sounds and the voice inside Woman's head vanish as we switch to his point of view.

Woman is alone, smoking meth at the door knob "coffee table" downstage. She hears:

FATHER'S VOICE You will die soon. You will *die.* You *deserve* to die. You're useless. What are you good for? Nothing. *Nothing!* NOTHING!

(Woman is startled out of her stuporous
haze. She looks around for the source
of the withering voice.)

FATHER'S VOICE   Never born, never born, never born,
I wish, I wish, I wish you were never born.

(Woman reacts to the oppressive,
negative energy.)

FATHER'S VOICE   You can't do that. You'll never finish. You're not smart enough. What makes you think
you could ever do that?

(Woman rushes to the wall and
starts banging on it, as if she has
found the location of the voice.)

WOMAN   Stop it! STOP IT!

FATHER'S VOICE   Silly girl! *(maniacal laughter)* Silly,
silly girl! Look at you!

(Woman rushes to a new section
of wall and bangs on it.)

FATHER'S VOICE   Have you looked at yourself? *Have
you?* Look in the mirror. You're a homely girl. Just
like your mother. Nobody will ever want you. So
come here. Come to your daddy.

(Woman runs to the stove and grabs
the frying pan. She runs back to the
wall and smashes a hole in it.)

FATHER'S VOICE   Oh, look, the ugly fuckling is quack-
ing up. Quack, quack, *QUACK!*

(Woman throws the pan across
the room, at the mocking voice.)

FATHER'S VOICE   You throw like a little bitch. Ding-dong, the bitch is dead. Ding-dong, the little bitch is dead, dead, dead.

(In a frenzy, Woman covers her ears.)

FATHER'S VOICE   That's it, little girl. That's right, nobody will hear a thing. You come to your daddy now. Come on. Daddy's got a surprise for you.

WOMAN   No!

FATHER'S VOICE   Oh yes he does. A very big, very hard surprise. So come on now. You're my sweet little girl. Don't worry, I'm not going to touch that ugly little face of yours — just bring those sweet little girl cheeks to daddy.

(Woman collapses to the floor,
behind the couch, trying to hide.)

WOMAN   No … please, daddy … no … please no!

FATHER'S VOICE   Get over here and get to work.

(Woman is dragged by her "invisible
father," feet first across the floor. She
shrieks, a high-pitched girl scream.)

(**Note on the "dragging" stagecraft:** It
takes us into Woman's hallucination.)

FATHER'S VOICE   Shut your mouth, girl! Or I'll shut it for you.

(Woman whimpers as her father
begins to touch her.)

(Key in front door. Door opens.)

(Gary enters. The lighting and sound
snap back to "normal" as we enter his
point of view.)

WOMAN   *(little girl voice)*   Please stop. *Please.*

(Gary sees Woman writhing on the floor,
fighting off her "invisible father.")

GARY   What in the hell? ... What's going on?

(Gary crosses to Woman and watches
for a while. Disgusted, he shakes his
head as she flops and flails around.)

GARY   What's the matter with you? ... Junkie tweaker
... You overdosed again, didn't you.

(He reaches for Woman.)

WOMAN   No! DON'T TOUCH ME!

GARY   Hey! You don't tell me not to touch you!

WOMAN   *(speaking to her "father")*   Get away! You're
drunk!

GARY   YOU'RE STUPID! ... GET UP!

(Woman remains on the floor,
twitching, flailing, crying.)

(A beat.)

(Gary drags Woman across the room,
back to her previous position. He starts
to pull her pants off. She fights back, but
she's exhausted. Her contortions slow.
Ready to submit, Woman goes limp.)

GARY   Jesus ... finally.

(Gary pulls Woman's jeans off and
throws them toward the fireplace.
He reaches for her underpants and
starts to peel them off.)

(Blackout.)

Scene 13

A flashback played behind a scrim, with backlighting,
so what we see are silhouettes.

Woman as a 12-year-old girl, cowering in her rollaway
bed as she listens to her parents' angry voices ricochet-
ing around. She covers her ears with her hands.

Sound design: As in the previous scene, the offstage
pre-recorded voices have a nightmare quality.

MOTHER   Get away! You're drunk!

FATHER   It's the only way I can stand to be around you!

MOTHER   Don't touch me! *Don't you touch me!*

FATHER   Get over here!

  (Sound of commotion, sudden
  thuds, a lamp is knocked over.)

MOTHER   Get out of this house!

FATHER   You're a worthless sorry whore. It's my house.
  Go back to the gutter where you belong.

MOTHER   I will. *I'll leave.*

FATHER   Go ahead. Good luck. You'll starve.

MOTHER   I'd rather die than stay here.

FATHER   You've got no place to go.

MOTHER   I don't care.

FATHER   You *need* me.

(A beat, then hysterical laughter from
Mother. Then a loud slap in the face,
a scream, and a punch. Then silence.)

12-YEAR-OLD WOMAN   Mommy! *Mommy!*

(When there is no answer, the girl begins to cry. The door to her bedroom is
kicked open; her drunken father busts
in. The girl cowers under the covers.)

FATHER   SHUT UP!

(Her father grabs the covers and rips
them off the bed. The girl screams.)

FATHER   I said, SHUT YOUR MOUTH, GIRL!

(Her father grabs an edge of the rollaway
bed and violently upends it, tossing the
girl onto the floor. She screams again.
Her father kicks her. She falls silent.)

FATHER   That's better. A child should be seen and not
heard. But you shouldn't even be seen. Now get in
there and clean up your mother — she can't even do
that by herself. And then get back in here.

(The girl rises off the floor, onto her
hands and knees, and begins to crawl
out of the room.)

(Lights fade to black.)

Scene 14

The house.

Gary is watching television. Woman enters from the
bedroom, carrying a bulging duffel bag. She sets it on
a chair by the dining table, which is still tipped over.
She sits in another chair and watches Gary watching
TV. After a while, he looks over at her.

GARY   What are you doing?

WOMAN   I don't know.

GARY   You don't know what you're doing?

WOMAN   No. I don't. But I know I don't want to be
   doing this.

GARY   This?

WOMAN   Yes. *This.*

GARY   It looks like you're just sitting there … doing
   your usual nothing Woman thing. Why don't you get
   up and do *something* for a change?

   (Woman thinks about the chances
   of success for her plan.)

WOMAN   A change … You're absolutely right … I
   should stand up and *do* something — for a *change.*

   (Gary goes back to watching TV.)

   (A long beat.)

WOMAN   I'm going to California.

GARY *(dismissive)* *You're* going to California …
Have you ever been there? What's in California?

WOMAN It's not what's there, it's what's *not* there.

GARY Whatta ya mean by that?

WOMAN I'm leaving. I can't do this anymore.

(Gary clicks the remote to turn
off the television.)

GARY What are you talking about? Whatta you mean,
this? You can't do *what* anymore?

WOMAN Are you kidding me?

GARY Why would you go to California? What for?
I have no idea what you're talking about.

WOMAN You know what? I don't think you do.
I don't think you've got a clue.

GARY You know what? You sound irrational.

WOMAN No. I'm as rational as I've ever been in my
entire life. I'm *going* to California. I'm leaving you,
Gary.

(A beat. Woman stands up, grabs the
duffel bag, and takes a couple of steps
toward the front door. Gary leaps up
and rushes over to block her path.)

GARY Whoa! Whoa! Whoa! What's the matter?

WOMAN Get out of my way.

GARY Baby, you can't go. You *need* me *(strategic
pivot)* and I need you.

WOMAN Unless things change, I don't need *this.*

GARY I still don't understand what you mean. What is *this?*

(A beat.)

WOMAN THIS HOUSE! THIS LIFE! *YOU!* YOU TREAT ME LIKE SHIT! YOU BROKE MY ARM!

GARY Jesus Christ! Now you're blaming *me* for that? Listen! I don't know what you think happened that night, but you were high as a freaking kite. *Higher!* But I'm not blaming you. We both were. If anything, we're both to blame for letting things get out of hand, for letting things go too far. Responsibility always cuts both ways. But this much I know: I *love* you. We're good together. Most of the time, we're *great* together. Why would you leave?

> (A long beat as Woman considers this version of their relationship. Then she tries to step around Gary to get out the door, but he moves, too, and blocks her path.)

GARY *Whoa, baby, wait!* Come on! What are you doing? What have you got to complain about?

> (Woman steps back and stares at Gary, trying to assess whether he's crazy or she's crazy. Or whether they both are. After a while, Gary reads her face and drops to his knees. He begins to beg.)

GARY Don't go. *Please don't go!* Tell me what to do and I will do it. I love you so much. I don't want to lose you. I don't want to lose what we have!

(A beat.)

WOMAN *(disbelief)* You love me.

GARY   I love you more than anything in the world! I would be lost without you. I'll do anything for you. I'll take all the blame for everything, if that's what you want. If you think things need to change, if you're truly unhappy, then I will change.

(A beat.)

WOMAN   You would change for me. For *us*.

GARY   Not "would." *Will*. Yes. I absolutely will.

(A beat.)

WOMAN   I don't believe you. What would you change? Where would you even start?

GARY   *(near tears)*   I don't know. I don't know what needs to change. But I'll start wherever you want me to. I *will* change. I will change whatever you tell me to. I promise.

(A beat.)

WOMAN   It's not just one thing … There are so many things that … *(cocks her head, perplexed)* You *really* don't know?

GARY   Make a list. Write them down. I can't make changes unless I know what you think is wrong. I'll work really hard. Baby, I love you so much.

WOMAN   A list.

GARY   Yes. Put everything on it. Whatever you want.

(A long beat.)

WOMAN   The first thing on my list would be this: STOP HITTING ME.

GARY   *(powerful; persuasive)*   I will never hit you again.

(A long beat as Woman evaluates.)

WOMAN OK … This is progress … This is good.

GARY See? It's not that hard. *(tentative)* Could I have a hug?

WOMAN *(wary)* I guess so.

> (Gary gets up off his knees. He and Woman embrace cautiously.)

> (Lights fade out.)

Scene 15

The house.

Woman is in the kitchen at the sink, washing the dishes. Gary is sitting by the door knob "coffee table" downstage, watching television before he leaves for work at the tattoo parlor. The dining table is still leaning, still broken, its leg has not been fixed. The steak knife is still stuck in the table top.

WOMAN Hey, Gary?

GARY Yeah.

WOMAN I was thinking about something.

GARY If this is about your back, *I already said I was sorry! How many times do I —*

WOMAN *NO!* We're *NEVER* talking about that again!

GARY *(subterranean burn)* … OK, then *WHAT?*

> (A long beat.)

WOMAN This girl I know asked me if I wanted to get together after she gets off work today.

(Woman has Gary's full attention now.
He shuts off the TV and turns to her.)

GARY What girl? Is she named *Dennis?*

WOMAN *No.* Janelle. She works at my old office.

GARY You don't work there anymore.

WOMAN No. I don't.

GARY Why would she want to get together with you?
And why would you want to get together with her?
What's the point?

(Woman realizes the situation is
hopeless. She says nothing, but she
exhales loudly, which says a lot.)

GARY I'm talking to you! I asked you three questions!

WOMAN I'm sorry.

GARY You *know* that when you ignore me, it really sabotages how we're supposed to be changing. You *know* that's one of the things on *my* list. Why do you do that?

WOMAN I wasn't thinking.

GARY You should think before you *don't* speak.

WOMAN OK.

GARY So tell me again: Who is this girl that wants to see you?

WOMAN Janelle. She works at the front desk.

GARY How did she get in touch with you?

WOMAN She called me.

GARY   Here? At the house?

WOMAN   Yes.

GARY   When?

WOMAN   Yesterday.

GARY   I didn't hear the phone ring.

WOMAN   You were at work.

GARY   How did she get the number here?

WOMAN   I don't know.

GARY   *(mimicking Woman, cocks his head)*   You *really* don't know?

WOMAN   ... No ... I guess they still had it in my personnel file or something. She didn't say how she got the number. It was out of the blue. She just called.

GARY   "Out of the blue." Right. Tell me again why she called.

WOMAN   She just wondered ... Gary, really, it was no big deal.

GARY   TELL ME AGAIN WHY SHE CALLED.

WOMAN   She was just thinking that, I don't know, we could get together for happy hour or something.

GARY   "We," meaning the two of you. You and Janelle.

WOMAN   I think so. She didn't really specify, but that's the impression I got. But it's not important. I wasn't that close to her when I was there, so there's no reason for me to see her.

GARY   That makes sense. Good thinking. You don't have the money for happy hour anyway. How did you leave it? Did you tell her you weren't interested?

WOMAN   I just said I would check and see if you and I have plans and call her back.

GARY   "Call her back" … that was stupid.

WOMAN   I'm sorry.

GARY   Why would you get yourself in a situation like that?

WOMAN   I don't know. I don't need to call her back. She'll understand that I couldn't make it. That we — you and I — have plans.

GARY   So that's OK with you. You don't mind.

WOMAN   No … It's not like we were friends.

GARY   I think that's best. And anyway, baby, we do have plans. I'll bring home some takeout tonight. I'll try to be home around 10 o'clock. We'll have ourselves a party. Right here. Just you and me.

WOMAN   That sounds like fun.

   (Blackout.)

Scene 16

The house.

We hear a key turning in the front door lock. Woman pushes open the door and flips the wall switch. Lights up. Woman enters. A moment later, Gary enters from the bedroom. Woman screams.

WOMAN   OH MY GOD! You *scared* me … What are you doing home?

GARY   What are you doing *not* home?

WOMAN   Nothing.

GARY   Where were you?

WOMAN   What do you mean?

GARY   Is "where were you?" a difficult question to understand?

WOMAN   No, I was just … surprised. I went out for a few minutes, that's all.

GARY   What for?

WOMAN   To get … some wine for our party tonight … I'm glad to see you, baby.

GARY   So where is it?

WOMAN   Where's what?

GARY   Are you nervous? Do you have something you want to tell me? Are you not thinking straight? Are you having trouble following me? Because I don't think I can make it any simpler for you. The wine. Where is the wine? The wine that you went out to get for our party tonight. I do not see any wine. So where is it? That is the question I'm asking you. *Where is the wine?* Should I write that down on a sheet of paper for you? Where … is … the … WINE?

WOMAN   I didn't get any. They didn't have any that I thought you would like, so, you know … Hey, why don't we start our party now? Why don't we have some fun? I'll make you feel real good. *So* good. I'll do anything you want.

GARY   I don't think so. Suddenly I'm not in the mood to party. I'm in the mood to hear a little more about this wine trip you took. Where did you go?

WOMAN   To that, oh, you know, that place on Broadway. We've been there together. You and me.

GARY   So, if I took you back there right now, they would remember that you were just there.

WOMAN   I think so. I mean, I didn't actually go up to the cash register, I didn't buy anything, but I think they would remember I was there.

GARY   And you're telling me they didn't have any wine that I would like. Not one single bottle. And nothing hard. They didn't have any Stoli or Jack. No Crown. No Cuervo. They didn't have *anything* we could party with.

WOMAN   Maybe they did. I don't know. I guess I wasn't sure. So I didn't get anything. If I made a mistake, I'm sorry, Gary. I am. If I did something wrong, I apologize. I will make it up to you. I will go back there right now and get whatever you want.

(Gary slaps Woman across the face.
She crumples to the floor.)

GARY   You lying little bitch! You goddamn little liar! GET UP!

(Woman starts to sob. She tries to
crawl away from Gary, but he grabs
her by the leg and pulls her back.)

GARY   Get up! Before I kick your lying teeth in!

(Woman struggles to get up. She grabs
hold of a chair to help with balance.
Finally she wobbles to her feet …)

(And Gary slaps her across the face
again, knocking her back down.)

(Woman is now struggling for survival.
She crawls toward a window, knowing
she must open it and flee. Gary watches
with cold, utter contempt.)

(Woman reaches the window, gets to
her knees, and places her hands on the
sill. Gary walks over and grabs her by
the hair, pulling her to her feet.)

GARY   Would you like some fresh air? Would that help
you to tell the truth?

(Gary grabs her head with both hands
and kisses her on the lips. Then he turns
her head toward the window. Woman is
silent, so Gary speaks for her.)

GARY   Yes, Gary, I would like some air … I've been
lying to you ever since I got home, so, yes, I think that
would help me to tell you the truth for a change. A
breath of fresh air would be nice. Thank you, Gary.
Thank you very much.

(Blackout.)

(We hear glass shattering.)

(An extra-long beat. Lights fade up.)

(The window is broken. Gary and
Woman are sitting on the couch,
downstage center.)

(Woman's face is bloody. She is barely
hanging on to consciousness.)

(Gary's left arm is around Woman's
neck, his hand gagging her mouth.)

(With his right hand, he is holding
a gun to her head.)

(Woman is crying, but not much
sound is able to escape.)

GARY   See, the thing is, when you lie to me, I'm going
to find out. I will *always* find out. That's why you
can't lie to me. Do you understand? ... I'm going to
take my hand off your mouth in a little minute, and
you better not yell or cry or scream or bitch or moan,
and I especially don't want you to lie to me anymore.
I just want you to nod if you understand ... If you
understand that you can't lie to me anymore ... Not
ever ... So think about that for the few seconds you
have left ... And then tell me you understand.

(Gary loosens his grip and pulls
his hand away from her mouth.)

WOMAN   (*gasping*) This ... is ... the truth ... I
swear to you ... I went out ... to buy wine.

(A beat.)

GARY   So that's the truth.

(Woman nods yes, but Gary wraps his
arm around her neck again, covering
her mouth so she cannot scream.)

GARY   YOU DIRTY LITTLE BITCH LIAR, THAT IS
NOT THE TRUTH!

(A beat.)

(Gary regains his composure. He cocks
the hammer on the pistol and presses the
barrel against Woman's head.)

GARY   See, the reason I know that is not the truth is, I didn't go to work today. No. I knew what you would do. I always know. Because I know you better than anybody else in the world. Just like you always wanted. I know you better than you know yourself. So I waited. And you did exactly what I knew you would do. I had faith in you. And you didn't disappoint me. You never do. I watched you leave the house. I followed you. I saw you meet Janelle. I hope you had a nice happy hour. I hope you're happy with how you're changing. I hope you're happy with what you've done to us.

> (Woman understands that she is about to be murdered. She starts to writhe and scream, but Gary subdues her, shoving her prone on the couch while keeping the cocked gun against her head.)

> (A long beat.)

> (Gary removes the gun from Woman's head. He uncocks the gun. He disengages from her. He stands up. Woman is confused, but she's too scared to be relieved.)

GARY   Hold that thought.

> (Gary puts the pistol in the waistband of his pants. He grabs a pillow off a chair. He goes to the kitchen and gets a dish towel. He returns to the couch. Woman is still lying there, petrified.)

GARY   Raise your head for me, baby.

> (She follows his order, and Gary slides the pillow under her head.)

GARY   Again.

(Woman raises her head, and Gary
places the dish towel on top of the pil-
low. He pushes her head back down,
onto the towel. Gary gently removes
Woman's glasses and places them on
the door knob "coffee table.")

GARY   I want you to relax. You don't need to see this.

(Gary pulls the pistol out of his waist-
band. He sits on the couch next to
Woman and pins her in place with his
body. The gun is in his right hand.)

GARY   Now open your mouth for me.

(A beat.)

WOMAN   Why?

GARY   I'm going to wash it out with soap … WHY
DO YOU THINK, YOU STUPID MORON. OPEN
YOUR LYING MOUTH!

WOMAN   Gary, my god … please … I am so sorry.
I'm sorry! *I'm sorry!* I'M SORRY!

(Woman realizes this is it and begins
to struggle for her life. But Gary is
too big and too strong. He finally
subdues her, and she lies limp.)

(A beat.)

(Gary cocks the hammer of the gun.)

GARY *(eerily calm)* I really wish I didn't have to do this … It makes me sad … We could have had such a long, wonderful life together … Now open your mouth for me.

(A beat.)

(Worn down, ready to accept her punishment, ready for her life with Gary to end, Woman does as she is told. Gary sticks the barrel of the gun into her mouth.)

GARY I love you so much, more than you will ever know, and this is how you treat me … Goodbye.

(Gary pulls the trigger. The hammer snaps down with a click.)

(But no shot rings out.)

(Gently, Gary removes the pistol from Woman's mouth. Strangely, Woman starts to weep because she is still alive. Gary places the pistol on the door knob "coffee table" and brushes hair away from her eyes. With the towel, Gary dabs at Woman's tear-stained cheeks.)

GARY I hope you've learned something, Woman … I hope you've learned that next time you lie to me, the gun is going to be *loaded* … Now come on, don't cry … Let's get started on our party. Remember, you said you're going to do anything I want tonight, so let's have some fun.

(Blackout.)

Scene 17

Downstage left, a light comes up to illuminate Woman, who is sitting in a chair. She is breaking the fourth wall with this monologue, but she is also telling herself the painful truth, facing up to her personal history, to the regrets and mistakes that she has buried, that she has never shared with anyone, because she has no friends. Ultimately, Woman has always been alone.

WOMAN   I never knew anything about sex. Americans are weird. Bipolar ... Schizophrenic ... Confused. We *hate* sex, but we *love* it. Our country should be called America, Land-of-the-I-Want-to-Get-Laid, Home-of-the-Lord-Jesus-I-Feel-So-Guilty ... We don't want to think about sex, but it consumes us. We can't talk about sex, but it's everywhere. It sells perfume, it sells jewelry, it sells clothes, it sells shoes, it sells makeup, it sells surgery, it sells cars, it sells books, it sells movies, it sells magazines, it sells video games, it sells cigarettes, it sells beer, it sells hotel rooms, it sells food, it sells toothpaste, it sells pretty much everything in this entire sex-crazed country ... If it wasn't for sex, our gross national product would be twenty-seven dollars. The United Sex of America ... It's insane. It's the elephant in the room with its trunk up our ass. I don't get it. It's everywhere, but we act like ... *(she shakes her head in wonderment)* ... What are we afraid of? That two people might beat the odds, fall in love, and do what would come naturally if they weren't messed up in the head? That some 14-year-old girl might have a baby and not be able to take care of it? ... OK, I understand that one.

I got my period when I was around 11. Of course, I didn't know what it was. I thought I was *dying*. I ran home with blood leaking down my legs like Niagara Falls. How does somebody *not* prepare you for that? My mom's reaction didn't help. She had this look on her face like I had leprosy ... I think she would rather that's what I had. *Leprosy*. Or leukemia. Or spinal meningitis. Or a brain tumor. Anything except bleeding "down there." I looked at her face and saw horror and disgust. I was sure that was *it*. I was going to *die*. And that was fine. It felt so peaceful ... I didn't have to do homework anymore. Not that I ever did much. No more history. No more biology. No more *nightmares* about biology ... No more dad. It was all going to end, finally ... No more *me* ... I was ... *relieved* ... I didn't have to hear them ... I didn't have to ...

(Woman remembers being molested
by her father and cannot speak. But
she puts that out of her mind, the way
she always has, and continues.)

It was ironic. Dying would give me back my life. I was going to be *free* ... free from *everything*. Except I didn't die. I just kept bleeding ... Sometimes, when I think back to when I was a kid, I wonder how I ever survived. Nobody told me *anything*. How did I learn what I learned? From other girls who didn't know anything. But I *really* didn't know anything. I knew *less* than nothing. Then I quit bleeding. Pregnant at 14. Uh-huh, that was me. Suddenly I was "daddy's stupid little slut." A little girl with a tiny daughter ... I don't know where she is ... She got given away, or something. Nobody told me anything about *anything*. That's what got me into trouble. With a neon capital T. Big red capital R. Capital O. Capital *everything*.

I remember the first time I ever heard the word. This neighbor kid named Timmy and I were walking home from the last day of school before summer vacation. And Timmy says, "So, you wanna fuck?" And I say, "Huh?" I distinctly remember saying, "Huh?" How is it that nobody prepares you for the first time a boy says, "You wanna fuck?" Shouldn't you be ready for that? Shouldn't you be prepared? Be prepared like the boy scouts? Maybe the girl scouts get you ready for that. I don't know. I never joined anything, so I was never a girl scout.

But shouldn't you have an *idea* of what fucking involves? Of what goes where? Of *why* it goes there? Like maybe you should know that around the time you can get pregnant? And how does a kid named Timmy learn about this? This thing called fucking? *Timmy?* Shouldn't *Timmy* be catching frogs at the creek? Or looking for some arrowheads in the woods? Or organizing his stamp collection? But this Timmy, who apparently has interests other than frogs and Indian artifacts and stamps, says to me *again,* after the "Huh?" … as if I hadn't heard him … Timmy says, "You wanna fuck?" And I say, "I guess so." … Wow … "I guess so." Some answer. If he had asked me if I wanted a piece of gum, my answer would have been the same.

(Blackout on Woman.)

(Downstage right, a light comes up on Gary, also sitting in a chair. He begins to describe his world, also breaking the fourth wall, as he justifies his need to dominate women. He believes everything he says is true. Only some of it is.)

GARY I fake everything. At least in the beginning. If there's anything real about me, I push it down — down so far that it can never reach the surface. A man shouldn't have to live this way. It's terrible. I have to be *so* careful. It makes me tired. I have to watch myself constantly. Otherwise I scare people … I scare *women* … They get that look on their face. I hate that look. I think I'm pretty normal, though. Everybody is like me … OK, maybe I don't know that for a fact, because you can't prove it, you can't just say to somebody, "Hey, you're faking it, right? You're just saying what you have to say to get what you want, right?" Even if you had them cold, if they *were* faking everything, they would have to deny it. They could never tell you the truth. If they don't admit it, then that makes *you* the weirdo, not them. That's what I believe. And I'm sure I'm right.

The first few times I got punched, my old man slugs me in the arm for no reason. Sure, he was drunk, but I think it was mostly because he could. He was way bigger than me. I never went down like a girl. *Never!* I stayed up. I *took* it, even though Dad hit you right on the bone … no muscle to soften the blow, just dock worker knuckles on fourth-grade bone. It was good training, though. It got me ready for the world. And I never hid. *Never!* … Later I got diagnosed with some "anger issues." Like that's a bad thing? When he told me that, when the prison shrink told me that, it was the most I ever laughed in my life. He looked at me through those big thick glasses, with those gigantic eyes, he looked at me like I was insane. And that made me laugh even harder. He had about ten college degrees on his wall, probably from online universities, but he didn't understand that if I wasn't angry about all the stuff that happened, I *would* be insane. I had a choice. I could stand around and take it and go crazy, or get angry and do something about it — *get control* — do it to them before they did it to me. Or after they did it to me. That's why I stabbed my ex-wife.

(Gary takes a hit off his meth pipe.)

It was just a little love tap … to get her back … She knew she deserved it … Those are the kind of people that move the world, the angry ones … If you wanna get listened to, if you wanna get results, if you wanna get what you *want*, you've got to get *angry*. Mr. Big Glasses talked about being "psychologically proactive," and that's exactly what I was — psychologically pro-active with a steak knife … It felt good.

(Blackout on Gary.)

(Light up on Woman.)

WOMAN   The first time I got raped … on a date … I actually thought it was sex. That's how stupid I was. That's probably why I didn't do it for a long time after that. I knew something was wrong, but I didn't know what. After that, I laid in bed at night and practiced stiffening up — like a board — so I could get through quote - sex - unquote … *if* I ever did it again. I guess I should say, if it was ever *done to me* again. God, I was such a terrible lay for such a long time. Later, I met a guy who showed me it didn't have to be like a war, like an invasion. Ha, you really could make *love*, not war. That was a revelation. Not the Bible kind, but the eye-opening kind. It was true, you could do it with your eyes open instead of putting on a blindfold.

(Woman takes a moment to think
about other men she has known.)

I had a few relationships … I guess they were relationships … But they didn't last. Dirty dishes and
dirty laundry always seemed to be a problem. Or
money. Or liquor. Or sex. Or drugs. Or friends. Or
TV. Or jobs. Or jealousy. Or sex. Or the toilet seat.
Or the trash. Or the dog. Or the parrot. Or leg hair.
Or underwear. Or sex. Or this. Or that … Or
maybe I just wasn't what they wanted … I wasn't a
girl out of a *magazine* … I never bleached my hair;
maybe I could have done better as a blonde … And
my body was very average … OK, *below* average …
Well below. I didn't have a single curve … I was like
Highway 50 across Nevada … Nothing of interest as
far as the eye could see, and beyond that, *below* the
horizon, more of the same … Plus, I wasn't pretty, at
least nobody ever told me I was, and I didn't think so
either. The mirror was *not* my friend. I should never
have read Glamour and Vogue and Cosmo. Those
magazines really tore me up. They kicked me right in
the head. Slapped me right in the face. I thought the
women in those magazines were real. And when I was
15, I understood I could never be one of them.

(Blackout on Woman.)

(Light up on Gary.)

GARY   There are people that think they can control
you. They think they can push you around … People
with certificates on their office wall … Yeah, like a
certificate from the University of Phoenix means
you're smarter than me. Hey, William O. Wonderass, I
guess you don't feel so smart now … now that you
have less teeth than me … oh, excuse me, *fewer* teeth
than me. I guess you're kinda surprised that my fist
has a GED. Women are like that, too. Do this, do
that. Be this, be that. *Don't* do this, *don't* do that.

Don't be this, *don't* be that. Where do they get their certificate? I don't know. Somewhere. Maybe from the school between their legs.

(Blackout on Gary.)

(Light up on Woman.)

(The sound perspective changes. We are hearing Woman think now. Her lips do not move. This is prerecorded audio, a stream-of-consciousness broadcast from inside her mind.)

(Woman's demeanor has changed, too. She hugs herself tightly. She has become smaller. She rocks back and forth like a traumatized child.)

WOMAN'S VOICE   I've got to end it. Somehow. Find a way out. Or he'll kill me. Or I could let him kill me. Get it over with. Maybe that's the way out. All the way out. *Punch* out. That would end it. Write a letter to … who? … to Janelle? … to … somebody … I'm involved with this … Involved? … I'm *married* to him. I'm his *prisoner.* I'm in his *jail* … He seemed OK for a while … and then not OK, not even close to OK … a suspicious, jealous, angry, violent son of a bitch. And I was so stupid … For a while, I thought it was my fault; for a while, I thought he would change … If I turn up dead, Gary did it. Gary killed me be-cause he could.

(Blackout on Woman.)

(Light up on Gary.)

(Agitated, Gary is pacing. We hear his thoughts, the same sound perspective as a moment ago for Woman.)

GARY'S VOICE   Woman's gonna leave. Gonna run, gonna run, gonna run. I oughta take a thousand dollars, go to Vegas, put it on the bitch getting the hell outta here. Even money. No, no, no ... that's no good ... I'd have to let her go to win the bet. But she's *not* getting outta here ... Funny thing is, if she stayed, everything would be fine. Love conquers, yeah, it does ... And love *kills*. If you leave, bitch, look out. Why do you think you can leave? Are you stupid? Are you *blind?* Do you not *see* that is the absolute worst thing you can do? You're branded. You're mine. Where do you go with that tatt? Who wants to look at that ink besides me? What, are you gonna find another Gary? I don't think so. You're not transfer-able. I'm all you've got. I'm all you'll ever have.

(Blackout on Gary.)

(Spotlight up on the bedroom door.
Woman emerges carrying her duffel bag
— full of clothing. She is dressed for
traveling. She goes to the kitchen and
stops. She looks at the dining table,
which is still tipped over. The steak
knife is still stuck in the table top.)

(Woman drops the duffel and stoops
to grab the table leg that broke during
Gary's no-rain dance. She lifts the table
and props the leg under it. She disap-
pears into the bedroom and returns with
a roll of duct tape. She wraps tape around
and around and around the table leg. She
tries to tear the tape but cannot. She goes
to a kitchen drawer and comes back with
scissors. She cuts the tape.)

(She puts the scissors in her jeans pocket.)

(She pats down the tape on the table leg
and steps back to look. The table remains
standing. She nods; she has fixed something. She tries to pull the steak knife out
of the table. It refuses to budge. She tries
again. Applying Arthurian effort, Woman
frees the knife, and maybe herself. She
returns the knife to the kitchen drawer.)

(Woman walks to the refrigerator and
opens its door. We hear her thoughts
in recorded voiceover.)

WOMAN'S VOICE Black bananas … I've eaten worse.
*(she throws them in the duffel bag, then smells a carton
of sour milk and reacts as if it's a dead skunk)* Oh my
God! *(she pours it in the sink, goes back to raiding the
fridge)* Yogurt. Should be all right. *(tosses a container
of yogurt into the duffel)* Half a jar of strawberry jam.
(tosses jam into duffel) And where would I be without
leftover pizza? That's a couple of lunches on the road.

(Woman wraps the pizza slices in tin foil
and puts them in the duffel bag.)

(Woman recalls something. She stands on
a chair to reach the top shelf in a kitchen
cabinet. She brings the large round metal
container down to the counter top, opens
it, and pulls out a chocolate bar. She rips
the wrapping off and takes a bite. It's a
singular moment of pure pleasure.)

(But now it's time for her to get moving.
Woman rewraps the rest of the chocolate
bar and throws it in the duffel bag. She

starts to put the round container back on the top shelf but changes her mind. She comes back down, with the container, and opens her duffel bag. She rearranges things to make room under the clothes, then pours the entire contents of the container into the bag: Dozens of chocolate bars. They flow like a waterfall.)

(Woman heads out the front door, leaving the house for, she thinks, the last time.)

(Outside, Woman shrieks.)

(The front door is kicked open by Gary, who carries Woman back into the house over the threshold, wedding-style.)

GARY   Remember the last time we did this?

(No answer from Woman.)

GARY   You know you're not getting out of here. You understand you can't leave, right?

WOMAN   What are you talking about, baby?

GARY   You weren't coming back.

WOMAN   Yes I was. Of course I was.

(Gary throws Woman, and her duffel bag, onto the couch. She assumes a fetal position.)

GARY   Oh, yeah? Where were you going?

WOMAN   To the store.

GARY   (*snorts*)   What? The *wine* store? ... Woman, do you know how much I love you? Do you have any idea?

WOMAN   I know you do. And I love you, too.

GARY   *(Knows she's lying)*   You do.

WOMAN   Yes.

GARY   I would do *anything* for you. Do you know that?

WOMAN   Yes. I absolutely know that.

GARY   Then why were you leaving?

WOMAN   I wasn' —

(Gary slaps Woman across the face.)

GARY   Shut up! *SHUT YOUR MOUTH!* Every time you open it, you lie.

(A beat. Gary considers Woman
as she cowers.)

GARY   Do you wanna tell me what's in the bag?

WOMAN   Gary, what are you doing home? Why are you not at work? Is something wrong?

GARY   No. Nothing's wrong. I don't work there anymore.

WOMAN   What? *What happened?*

GARY   You happened. I had to quit. Because now I have to watch you 24 hours a day.

(Gary grabs Woman's hair with one
hand and makes a fist with the other,
threatening to hit her.)

GARY   Tell me: WHAT'S IN THE BAG?

WOMAN   *(terrified)*   Please, baby, it's not what you think.

(Gary punches Woman in the face.
The blow knocks her unconscious.)

(Gary lets go of her hair. He shakes his
fist out, massages it a little. The blow
was painful to him, too.)

(Gary grabs a chair and sits before
Woman. He picks up the duffel bag,
places it on his lap, opens it. One by
one, he throws items of food across
the room, aiming for the kitchen sink.
He misses with most of them.)

(Gary pulls a piece of paper out of the
bag. He looks it over.)

GARY   Oh, this is funny. This is so funny. Nothing's
checked off. Guess what. Nobody likes lists of how
they're supposed to change. Not even you.

(Gary takes a lighter out of his pocket. He
holds the list up and lights it on fire. After
a few seconds, he drops it on the floor and
stamps out the flames with his shoe.)

(Gary goes back to rummaging through
Woman's duffel bag.)

(Then he sees the chocolate bars. He
shakes his head in disgust.)

GARY   You goddamn thief. Now you're just being
spiteful.

(Gary stands up and goes to the kitchen.
He retrieves the metal container from the
counter top where Woman left it, and comes
back to the duffel bag. He puts all of the

chocolate bars back into the container and returns it to the cabinet, on the top shelf.)

(He starts to walk back to Woman, then notices the table leg has been taped up.)

GARY   Oh, hey, nice. Thanks for fixing the table, baby. Good job.

(Gary gives the table leg a vicious kick and breaks it. The table buckles.)

(Gary walks back to Woman and stands over her. He crosses his arms.)

GARY   Woman, what are we gonna do with you?

(Gary remembers what she said about having lousy vision. He gently takes off her glasses and tries them on. He looks around. He looks at Woman. He will never see the world the way she does. He angrily throws the glasses out the window — the window that he shattered with Woman's head. He sits down and begins taking her clothes out of the duffel bag.)

(When he has gathered a pile of garments on his lap, he takes them to the fireplace and throws them in.)

(He turns on the gas to burn the clothing.)

(He also places the tip of a fireplace poker into the flames, to begin heating it.)

(He watches the fire.)

(A long beat.)

(Woman stirs. She moans. She raises
herself groggily. Gary takes note.)

GARY Hey, baby-maybe ... are we feelin' better now?

(Woman struggles up, getting to her
feet, and backs away, putting distance
between herself and Gary. Without
her glasses, she steps carefully, feeling
her way along, touching objects to
keep her bearings and balance.)

WOMAN If you kill me, you'll go to prison. *Back* to
prison.

GARY Where do you get these crazy ideas? Have you
gone insane? I honestly think you've lost your little
mind. Nobody's killing anybody. You and me, we're
forever ... But if I do kill you, I'm not going back to
prison, I promise you that. Prison is no place for a
sane person ... Maybe you'd do all right.

(Woman takes a couple of stealthy steps
toward the front door. Gary moves quickly
to cut off her angle. She stops. He pulls a
chair in front of the door to block it off.)

(A beat.)

GARY But we *are* going to have to make a few simple
changes. I'm sure you understand how that works ...
Do you understand? If you do, speak now. *Open your
mouth for me* ... and speak.

(A beat.)

WOMAN Yes. I understand. And I just need to get out
of here for a day or two, clear my head, and then we'll
make those changes. OK? Do you understand that?

GARY   See, that's the first simple thing we have to change. We have to figure out a way for you to not be stupid. There's no "getting out of here." You're stupid if you don't understand that. You're very ignorant. You're not thinking. You *have* lost your mind. How many times do I have to explain it to you? You don't listen.

WOMAN   I listen.

GARY   Will you throw me the oven mitt, please?

WOMAN   What?

GARY   See? You don't listen.

WOMAN   The oven mitt?

GARY   Yes, that's what I said. Do I need to write it down for you? In easy-to-read block letters? Sky-write it in the sky? Do a PowerPoint presentation? GIVE ME THE OVEN MITT! ... Please.

> (Reacting to Gary's mind games, Woman moves angrily to the kitchen and grabs the steak knife from the drawer. She also gets the oven mitt. She turns to face Gary and takes a few steps toward him. She raises the oven mitt, in her right hand, and the knife, in her left hand.)

WOMAN   Your choice, Gary.

GARY   *(cool, calm)*   I'll take the oven mitt ... Please.

> (Confused, but with adrenaline flowing, Woman throws Gary the mitt, *hard*.)

GARY   Thank you. Now, where were we? Oh, yes, the second simple thing. The second simple thing is, who belongs to who? We have to change your concept of what that means. You're very loose with the definition of "belonging." Basically, you're just *loose*. Then again, maybe you know you're mine. Then another again, maybe I made a mistake before. Maybe I put the tatt on the wrong side. Maybe you just need a new reminder — that *you* can see. Another *permanent* reminder. A rebrand ... Something meaningful ... How about a nice scar? A scar would be good. A *deep* scar would be *very* good, a symbol you'll be proud of. You'll look at it every morning in the mirror. Touch it ... Feel the texture ... Appreciate the beauty of the discoloration ... Remember this night ... The thing about scars, you never forget how you got them. Or why. You *learn* from them. You'll learn to love your scar. It'll be there for you every day. Like I am. *You* may be a liar, but the mirror isn't.

(A beat.)

WOMAN   *Fuck the mirror!* ... *AND FUCK YOU!*

GARY   We'll get to that. But first I'm going to give you that special something — that special *something else* — to remind you of our bond ... that we'll be together for as long as we both shall live. You know, like we said. Remember that? Do you remember our vows? I take them seriously. And you should, too. I'm going to help you remember them. So drop the knife — the knife that I told you never to touch — and let's move forward with our relationship. Take the next step. Let's *learn* something about each other. Let's *change*. Just like you always wanted.

WOMAN   Gary, I love you. I *do* ... You know that, don't you? I just need a little break. Some time to myself. I'm begging you. Time to get straightened out. And then we'll start fresh. Like we were in the beginning. Remember Point A? Can we just start over? At Point A? That first month? And yes, I remember our vows. And yes, I take them seriously.

GARY   I want you to prove it ... by putting the knife down.

(A beat as Woman considers.)

WOMAN   If I put the knife down, can we start over? Please, baby.

GARY   You've let me down in so many ways. How can I trust you? You're a liar. You've lied about so many things — lie after lie after lie — how can *you* even trust what you tell yourself about *me?* Everything you touch, you destroy. *Everything!*

WOMAN   You can trust me ... I'll prove it to you. But you've got to prove something to me, too. Show me you still love me. Show me you won't hurt me. Show me you won't hit me. Like you promised.

(A beat.)

GARY   OK ... that's fair. You show me something, I'll show you something.

(A long beat.)

(Woman turns around, her back facing downstage. She unbuttons her shirt and lowers it to reveal the tattoo.)

WOMAN   I'm yours. I belong to you. Just like it says: Property of Gary. This tattoo is the truth. This tattoo is forever. Just like we are.

(A beat.)

(Woman drops the knife on the floor.)

GARY You're the best work I've ever done. Yes. Now we can move forward.

> (Woman puts her shirt back on and turns around to face the man who has abused her for so long. Gary moves to the fireplace and, wearing the oven mitt, picks up the poker. Its tip is glowing red. Unable to see very well, Woman doesn't understand what's about to happen. Gary advances toward her. When they are nearly face to face, he raises the glowing fireplace poker and points it at Woman's face.)

GARY This is going to hurt.

> (Now Woman understands. She pulls the scissors from the right front pocket of her jeans.)

WOMAN This, too.

> (Lights slam down to near blackout.)

> (Gary screams. He drops the fireplace poker and falls to the floor, clutching his stomach.)

> (The brightly glowing tip of the fireplace poker is nearly the only thing we can see. Woman grabs the poker and raises it.)

> (The red-hot tip floats above Gary.)

> (The potential for more violence is frozen in tableau for a moment.)

> (Then the glowing poker comes down, sizzling against Gary's face. He screams again. Woman tosses the poker across the room. She bolts for freedom. She moves

(the chair away from the front door, flings it
open, and she is gone.)

(In the dim light, we cannot see much.
Mostly we hear Gary breathing and moan-
ing. He pulls the scissors out of his gut
and throws them against the wall.)

(Gary crawls toward the telephone on a
stand near the front doorway. He keeps
one hand on the wound, trying to stop
the flow of blood. He pulls himself up
and dials 9-1-1 with his free hand.)

GARY   Help me, please help me, I've been stabbed …
yes, 614, on the corner … my wife … no, she ran
off, she's gone, she smokes a lot of meth, I've tried and
tried, but I can't get her to stop … she stabbed me in
the stomach … scissors … yeah, and she burned my
face … fireplace poker … she's a dangerous junkie,
completely paranoid, she went crazy … the things she
said, totally crazy … out of nowhere, I didn't see it
coming, no warning … thank you, please hurry, I'm
really bleeding … the front door is open … I'm going to lie down till they get here … thank you, and
please tell them to hurry.

    (Gary drops the phone, and it dangles
    by the cord. He slumps to the floor,
    lying in the doorway.)

    (Lights dim even more, to blackout, as
    we hear a police siren, getting closer,
    louder.)

    (Soon, a police car pulls up outside
    the house.)

(Its rotating light sends scorching red beams in through the open front door, illuminating Gary intermittently.)

(The police siren fades down. The red light keeps flashing through the front door.)

(The flashing police light finally fades to black.)

Scene 18

In the dark, from on high, we hear a booming voice:

JUDGE The defendant may address the court.

(A spotlight comes up to reveal Woman, sitting in a courtroom chair. She stands, tentatively, looks around at her surroundings, gathers a few thoughts, and begins.)

WOMAN My name is Sarah ... Sarah Lillian Robinson ... I'm just going to say that. Like they say, for the record. It's been about ... I don't know ... Five years? Ten years? Since anybody said my name. Since anybody even knew who I was, knew that I existed. And even when I existed, if you can call it that, I didn't really exist. I was a ghost. I was as close to dead as you can be, and still be alive ... I know what I did was wrong ... but that doesn't mean ...

(A beat.)

You know what? It was *right*. It was him … or it was me. For the first time in my life, I chose *me*. At that moment, if you had been married to Gary, if you had … endured the … insults … the ridicule … the slaps, the punches, the fear … the feeling that you would … rather be dead … that you *deserved* to be dead, then anybody in this courtroom might have done what I did … I lost it … And then I found it … Survival. That's what I'm guilty of … surviving.

Maybe I could have run, or should have run, when it first started … Why didn't I think of that? The thing is, you don't think. You can't think. You don't have the ability to think. You just exist. You just *are*. And you wonder whether you are *not*. You're waiting. For the next fist. For the next handful of hair yanked out of your head. For the next kick … You're waiting for him to change … When I finally understood that *he* was the liar, when I finally understood he would *never* change, when I finally *tried* to run, it was too late.

When somebody tells you they love you, all the time, and nobody has ever told you that, not in your whole life, you *hope*. You want to believe. When he gives you all those roses … and a ring …

(A long beat as Woman remembers and starts to cry a little. But she ignores her tears and pushes onward.)

You *do* believe … until he smashes your head through a window … until he breaks your arm … And then you're just confused. It's *completely* confusing. You ask him, "Why did you do that?" And he says, "Because I love you too much" … If that's not confusing, then nothing is. It didn't *feel* like love. It felt like a face full of glass. It felt like a broken arm. It felt like a shattered cheekbone. I *know* what those things feel like. They *hurt.* I don't think love is supposed to feel like that. I hope not. Maybe three years in prison is going to feel like freedom. I hope so. I would laugh. That would be funny. Irony has a way of tapping me on the shoulder and then punching me in the face … Three years of "freedom" *(she uses air quotes)* … Maybe I'll feel like I belong to nobody but myself.

Above all, I'm going to remember this day, and these years … and *those* years … for a long, long time. And then … someday … I hope to forget them … I guess that's all … Thank you.

> (Woman turns, puts her hands behind her back, and waits. Handcuffs are put on her wrists. She begins to shuffle out of the courtroom.)

GARY I'll be there when you get out. We'll start over. We'll go back to Point A.

> (Woman turns back to look. A light reveals Gary, sitting in a chair in the back of the courtroom.)

GARY I forgive you. *(he stands up)* Because I still *love* you. And I know you love me … You and me, *Sarah* … FOREVER!

> (A long beat.)

WOMAN I got it removed … All that's left is a purple scar … And that's already beginning to fade.

> (Woman turns away from Gary and continues offstage.)

> (Lights fade to black.)

> (Curtain.)

Cascadia Press

www.ingramcontent.com/pod-product-compliance
Lightning Source LLC
Chambersburg PA
CBHW030643130626
46552CB00002B/993